# THE PHANTOM BIRD AND OTHER STORIES

# INDUS FICTION

# The
# *Phantom Bird*
## and Other Stories

## Jai Nimbkar

*An imprint* of HarperCollins *Publishers* India

INDUS

An imprint of HarperCollins *Publishers* India Pvt Ltd
7/16 Ansari Road, New Delhi 110 002

Published by Indus 1993

© Jai Nimbkar 1993

ISBN 81–7223–058–3

Typeset in 10/11 Baskerville by
Tulika Print Communication Services (P) Ltd

Cover design by Bipul Guha

Printed in India by
Swapna Printing Works (P) Ltd.,
52 Raja Rammohun Roy Sarani
Calcutta 700009

# ACKNOWLEDGEMENT

I am indebted to the following magazines for publishing the stories in the present collection: *Imprint* for "The Phantom Bird"; *Eve's Weekly* for "Peanuts for the Monkeys"; *Femina* for "Ask No Questions", "Distorted Heaven", "The Huntress", "The Other Woman", "The Hunt", "Turning Points", "Night Sounds", "A World of Your Own", "The Torturer", and "The Childless One"; *The Illustrated Weekly of India* for "The Death of a Hero"; *Quest* for "A Friend of the Family"; and *Thought* for "Cross-Cultural Communication".

JN

# CONTENTS

# THE PHANTOM BIRD

## 1

The driver was not really reckless, but almost any speed would have seemed reckless as the taxi wound along the narrow road cut precariously into the mountainside. On the left was the overhanging mountain which, if it had been only a few inches lower, Sagar thought, would surely have touched the top of the Fiat, and on the right the laughing Beas river far below them. Suddenly around a curve a truck confronted them. Neither vehicle had given a warning hoot, and the taxi rattled so much that nobody had heard the approach of the truck. Sagar heard her mother's gasp through the screech of the two sets of brakes. She looked at the driver's impassive face as he backed cautiously to a place which was wide enough for the truck to pass. Maybe, she thought, driving in these parts required one to be fatalistic. Her father implored the driver to drive slower, and the driver replied that he was already driving slowly, that if he drove any slower they could not hope to reach Manali by nightfall. Sagar caught the slight amusement in his tone. Suddenly she began to enjoy herself. She leaned back in the front seat and stretched her legs. "I think it's the most exciting drive," she remarked.

Rohini, still recovering from the shock of the near-accident, thought that it was exactly the kind of remark she would have expected Sagar to make. She suppressed her irritation. She was tired from the long day on the road, and would have liked just to lie back and close her eyes and allow herself to relax. But on this road it was impossible. Of course not that she could do anything to avoid an accident, it was just that if there was going to be an accident, she preferred to be awake to meet it.

She smiled a little as she told Gautam this rather morbid thought.

"If you want to sleep," he said, "I'll promise to stay awake."

"No, I don't think that will help. It's nothing rational, it's just an instinctive fear that you can't reason away like that."

"Are you really afraid?"

"Not seriously. Still, I don't trust the man's driving. He is the smart-alecky type who would take unnecessary chances just to show off."

"He's all right, he's not really taking any risks."

Their voices went on and on and Sagar thought, how can anyone talk so much? She shut out the words but the drone of the voices continued. Especially her mother's voice, slightly husky and so well-modulated. It didn't sound real, for God's sake. Civilized. Ever since Nitin introduced the word it had kept recurring in Sagar's thoughts. "Your mother is the most completely civilized person I have ever met." She would have been pleased at the compliment, even though it had not been meant to be one.

Sagar started a conversation in her atrocious Hindi. After seeing so many Hindi movies, she thought, one would at least expect me to speak fluent Hindi. But words and verb forms kept eluding her. She discovered that the driver's name was Harbhajan Singh, that he came from a village near Gurdaspur, that he owned the taxi in partnership with a cousin, that he was married and had two children.

Rohini said, "Sagar, you mustn't pry into his personal life."

"This is not prying."

"Anyway, you are distracting him. Let him keep his mind on the road."

Sagar knew exactly what her mother meant. What she objected to was her being chummy with the driver.

She said, "You are supposed to talk to a driver to keep him from falling asleep. And he doesn't mind my talking to him, do you?"

10

"No," the driver said.

"You can understand English?"

"*Thoda thoda.*"

Sagar burst out laughing. "Here I've been knocking myself out trying to speak Hindi and all the time you knew English."

She went on laughing and the driver responded with a polite smile.

Rohini said, "Sagar, please stop it," and Sagar stopped laughing as though a switch had been flicked off. She knew she had overdone it a bit.

In the silence that followed Rohini said, "Oh Gautam, just look at that gorge. Isn't it spectacular?"

Although Sagar had decided to ignore her mother's running commentary on the countryside, she half-rose in her seat and leaned over for a look. The gorge had suddenly deepened, and the outcrop of rocks made it look quite scary, she thought.

Rohini saw Sagar leaning behind the driver, her too-large breasts almost touching his shoulder, and thought, "My God, she is an animal." The grossness of it sickened her. She said, in a quiet, deadly voice, "Sagar, don't lean across like that. You can cause a bad accident."

As the road dropped down to the river, the valley slowly widened. The mountains didn't quite seem to press in on them from both sides. The driver stopped near a stream which flowed out of a rocky outcrop. He checked the water in his radiator, filled a plastic carbuoy with water, washed his hands and face, and, cupping his hands to the rock, drank his fill.

"This is good mountain water, if you want a drink," he told Sagar.

It had been a hot and dusty ride. She splashed her arms and face with the deliciously cool water and drank greedily.

She said, "This is lovely. Very refreshing, Mummy. Do you want a wash?"

Rohini said stiffly, "I can wait till we get to Manali."

11

Sagar got back into the car and the tiredness of the journey suddenly caught up with her. She slept and did not know how much later it was that the stopping of the car woke her. For a moment she was confused. Then the sensations crowded in on her. It was quite dark, and she could see stars in the sky. The air was fresh and cool and fragrant with something she could not name.

"Are we there?" she asked.

"Yes," Gautam said.

She got out of the car and stretched, luxuriating in the coolness of the night. The driver helped them unload the luggage, and then Gautam paid him and he said *Namaste* and turned away. Sagar thought this rather a cool and businesslike parting. After being together a whole day, there should be something more.

She said, "Good-bye, and thank you for bringing us here."

He turned back to her with a sudden eye-crinkling smile and said, "*Namaste ji.*"

Rohini said, "Come on Sagar. It's late. Don't you want to eat?"

Sagar waved to the driver and went in.

Rohini said, "You have no sense of proportion."

"What have I done now?"

"Why make such a production out of saying good-bye to him?"

"Well, after all, he did drive us all day, and just paying him off seemed a little rude, that's all."

"He wouldn't have had to drive us all day if his car hadn't broken down."

"That wasn't his fault."

"Perhaps not, but we suffered for it all the same."

"He suffered as much as we did. More, because he could have made more money if he had been able to reach here earlier."

Rohini didn't say anything.

Sagar noticed that the scent that was on the air had intensified in the house.

"Daddy, what's this smell?"

"It's pine."

"Why is it stronger in the house?"

"Because it's built of pine wood."

"What an absolutely lovely idea, to build something out of wood which smells so nice, rather than out of cement concrete."

"They build it out of pine because it's the cheapest material available, silly."

Sagar bit into a sandwich and found that she was very hungry. She always marvelled at the pleasure one could get out of eating.

"But why call it a log hut?" she asked.

"Obviously because it's built with logs," Rohini said peevishly. She felt too tired to tackle more than a few mouthfuls of food. There were violet shadows under her eyes and her mouth sagged slightly at the corners. After a long day of sparring with Sagar, she felt her patience at the snapping point.

Sagar said, "I mean, why hut? It's so insulting."

"To whom?"

"To the people who really live in huts."

"You do have a devious mind."

"It's not me that has a devious mind."

Gautam saw the storm warnings. He said to Rohini, "Why don't you go to bed, darling? You look very tired."

The gentle protectiveness of his tone scraped Sagar's nerves raw. She felt suddenly oppressed by the idea of spending four whole weeks with her parents in this confined space, in the closeness a holiday imposes. She thought she would scream if subjected any longer to anyone's company.

She said, "Why don't you go to bed too, Daddy? I'll clean up here."

"Well, all right, if you're sure. Good night. And don't stay up late. I am going to walk you off your legs tomorrow, so see that you get a good night's rest."

"Sure."

The heartiness of his voice jarred on her as much as the earlier gentleness had. It's all skin-deep, she thought. Fake words to express fake feelings. They have made do with them for so long that they have convinced themselves it's all real.

She rinsed out the thermos and the few dishes they had used and wiped the crumbs from the table. She saw a small mouse, its beady little eyes peeking at her from a hole in the corner of the kitchen. She laughed. "Sorry friend, there's nothing for you to eat here," she said as she turned off the kitchen light.

She walked past her parents' firmly closed door and unaccountably thought of a long-ago Sunday afternoon. They had played rummy after lunch. It was such a rare event and Sagar was enjoying it so much that she wanted it to go on and on, but Gautam and Rohini soon tired of it and retired to their room for a nap. Suddenly at loose ends, Sagar wandered disconsolately about the flat. She was startled by the sound of the doorbell, and opened the door to let in a friend of hers, a girl who lived in the same building. She was in tears and Sagar asked, "What's the matter?"

"My Daddy and Mummy are fighting."

This was nothing new. Sagar said, "So?"

"It's really bad this time. I got scared. I think he's going to kill her."

Sagar said, with the wisdom of an extra year behind her words, "Husbands don't kill wives just because they fight with them, silly." After she had succeeded in consoling the girl she said superiorly, "My Daddy and Mummy never fight. They love each other." As though offering corroboration of her statement, she looked at the locked door of their bedroom. She knew it was locked because she had tried it, and when it did not give, moved away from it fast, her heart pounding with shame and fear, because she knew it was something she ought not to have done.

## 2

Gautam felt desperately tired. It had been a very long day. They had left Chandigarh at daybreak, hoping to reach Manali for a late lunch. But the taxi had had a breakdown and there had been endless waiting, and it had finally taken them fifteen hours to get here. The hot shower relaxed his stiff limbs and left him pleasantly drowsy. But when he emerged from the bathroom and noticed that Rohini was crying, he put off the moment of total relaxation.

"Chilly, isn't it?" he said, getting under his blankets.

She refused to be coaxed into an ordinary conversation.

He said, "What's the matter?"

"Why is Sagar so horrid to me?"

He sighed. They had been over this before.

"It's just her age. She doesn't mean to behave badly with you particularly. It's just her way of working off tensions."

"I don't see her working off her tensions on you. With me she never lets up. She worries about being rude to a taxi driver whom she'll probably never see again, but she doesn't care how rude she is to me. I don't even know how to talk to her any longer. I wish I had never thought of this holiday. Obviously it's not going to work out the way I hoped."

"Come now, darling. You haven't even given it a chance yet. You are tired and you know being tired always makes you feel depressed. Try and sleep. I am sure you will feel different tomorrow."

Words, Rohini thought. I don't want words and explanations. I simply want him to hold me in his arms and make me forget my misery. She immediately thought, what's happened to me? I've never sought unquestioning support and solace from anyone.

"Hush, Ro, you mustn't cry," he said. "These walls are very thin. Sagar will hear you."

As soon as he said it, he thought it was ridiculous to let your child impose on you restrictions which make it impossible for you to behave naturally. But ever since Sagar was old enough to understand, he had felt constantly conscious of her presence and so deprived of privacy.

He had always wondered what suddenly made Rohini want, after twelve years of marriage, to have a child. They had decided that they didn't want children. They were perfectly happy in themselves. He had a reasonably large income from inherited investments, and felt no need to work for a living. He often congratulated himself that he had not succumbed to the temptation to join the rat race and make still more money. He wrote poetry and edited a bimonthly literary magazine which had a select limited readership. Rohini helped him with the magazine, bullied him gently when he slacked off in his writing, and gave wonderful parties to which people felt privileged to be invited. Their life was complete. They couldn't see how children could possibly add to it in any way, and they were not going to have children simply because it was the expected thing to do. Once when the relatives had all gathered together for a family wedding and Rohini was being badgered as usual, Rohini had said, pushed finally beyond the limit of the patience with which she usually handled such attacks, "There's no law that every couple must have children, is there?"

A cousin had said, "No, there's no such law, but apart from the danger of the extinction of the species, if all of us thought like you, most marriages would fall apart if there were no children." To which Rohini had responded acidly, "If children are the only thing that keeps a marriage together, it's not worth saving."

And then suddenly, inexplicably, she had wanted a child. He had never asked her why. He had taken it for granted that she had ultimately felt the need to assert her fecundity, whether for her own benefit or for others' he did not know. He had only felt a little hurt that she had not even consulted him when she took the decision. Had she been afraid that he would not agree? Listening to her sniffling, he was tempted to tell her that these problems were of her own making. Why should she expect him to help? Then, feeling a little guilty of his unworthy thought, he went over to her bed. She clung to him with an intensity which for a moment made him recoil. But in spite of himself a part of him responded in the familiar learned way. He said her name like a question, a demand.

"Not tonight, Gautam. I am bleeding."

Trying to recover his balance he said, "Again?"

"I suppose the strain of the trip started it."

"Shouldn't you see a doctor?"

"I don't think that's necessary. First of all, there probably isn't a doctor worth the name in this place. And I saw Dr Bhalla before we left Bombay. He said there's nothing to worry about. There are often long bleeding episodes before it stops altogether."

Gautam felt an overpowering repugnance. Rohini felt his sudden withdrawal and knew why. Despite their closeness, they had never talked freely about their bodily functions. There had never seemed any need. She had felt a need for the first time when she was pregnant, to share with him the changes in her body, the various new sensations she experienced. But she discovered that he was far from receptive. She had once asked him whether he would like to attend her delivery and he had expressed utter horror at the idea. Although she had been hurt and baffled by his extreme reaction, later she had been relieved. She felt that if he actually

17

had seen her in that totally vulnerable and ridiculous state, giving birth to a baby, she could not have faced him afterwards. It would have changed their relationship.

Gautam moved to his bed and she, dry-eyed now, listened to the little rustling sounds as he settled himself into a comfortable position.


3


Sagar opened her eyes to bright light. She had not pulled the drapes across the tall wide window. This was one of the things which always irritated her mother. "Darling, people in the next building can see everything when the light is on." Sagar always said, "If they are that interested, they can look. I don't care." She was no exhibitionist. She just didn't like the closed-in, airless feeling pulled curtains gave a room. Occasionally she had gone into her parents' bedroom before the bed was made and the room opened up in the morning, and wondered how they could stand the staleness of the air.

She saw by her watch that it was only five-thirty, but she felt completely rested, restless with energy. She felt a rising excitement as she looked at the view offered by her window, of majestic deodars and behind them, rising tall and distant and snow-covered, the Himalayan peaks. She drew in a long breath and slowly expelled it. If this were a story, she thought, I would pinch myself to make sure I am not dreaming. I am really here. In the Himalayas. They exist. And they look just like the calendar pictures.

She felt she couldn't stay indoors a moment longer, and changing into a pair of jeans and a sweater she slipped out, hoping that neither of her parents would hear her. It seemed important to get her first taste of this place by herself.

She followed an uphill road past some of the other huts, and found that it wound around and led up a hill. Early as it was, she met a stream of loggers coming down the hill. They carried their loads strapped to their backs instead of on their heads as she had seen people do at home. Most of them seemed young, with smooth faces and flat noses and slanted eyes. She thought they looked cute. One of them broke into a Hindi film song when he saw her. In Bombay she would have been angry if someone did that, but now it somehow gave her a good feeling that she had travelled hundreds of miles to come here and hear someone singing a song she had hummed dozens of times. She smiled at him.

The trail she was following led to a logging camp. By the time she was within sight of it she had begun to feel tired. She sat down to rest, watching the activity in the distance — the sound of axe and saw on wood, the rhythmic movement of bodies, men's voices chatting, an occasional warning shout followed by the reverberating sound of a series of logs being rolled down a slope to the spot where the carriers would pick them up. She felt sorry to see the tall handsome trees being converted into logs, but there was something vibrant in the scene, the woods and the men working and the heady scent of pine thick in the air, which moved her strangely.

After a while she looked at her watch idly and then thought, Oh my God, it's nearly two hours since I started and I had meant it to be only a short walk. Mummy's going to just eat me alive. She started running down the hill.

Rohini had wakened, contrary to expectation, refreshed and cheerful. It must be the weather, she thought. It's so fresh and cool and unpolluted. Gautam was still asleep and she went to see if Sagar was awake, feeling suddenly a wave of affection of her daughter, a need for her companionship. She promised herself that she was going to be more patient and understanding. Sagar's empty bed caught her off balance. And some time later when Sagar burst into the house at a run, breathless, with glowing cheeks and shining eyes, more nearly pretty than she had ever looked, Rohini felt cheated. It was as though Sagar had unwrapped a gift she had brought without waiting for her to show it off.

Sagar braked herself sharply and said, "Mummy, you're up early."

Rohini said, hearing her own voice cold and hard, "It's not early. Have you seen what time it is? Where on earth have you been? I was so worried."

"I only went for a walk. I meant to be back soon, but it took longer than I thought."

"You really shouldn't wander about alone. Especially so early in the morning. It might not be safe."

"But there were lots of people about. Log-carriers. I even talked to one of them."

"That's what I mean."

"You mean these people might do something to me?" Sagar said in an incredulous voice.

"Don't be literal."

"What *do* you mean then?"

Rohini felt the rising anger throbbing at her temples and turned away without answering.

4

They had quite a long walk through the woods and were resting on a small hill overlooking a stream. On the far side of the stream mountains stretched to the horizon.

Rohini said, "The snow peaks and the dark pyramidal deodars make such a beautifully structured scene. It's like living poetry."

Sagar didn't say anything. She thought, anyone else would have simply said, aren't the mountains beautiful? If they had to talk about it, if talking was the only way they could enjoy things, that's all they would have said. But not my mother. She is incapable of an honest reaction in honest words. Sagar sometimes thought Rohini must rehearse the phrases she inserted so casually into the conversation, like a comedian who rehearses all his extempore jokes. And behind the beautiful words there is nothing. Just nothing. She makes words do the work of feelings, and so devalues the things she talks about.

There had been a time when Sagar had listened raptly to discussions in their living room, in the course of which people talked about whether a writer might be judged just as a writer or must be judged as a black American writer of the twentieth century, or speculated anxiously about the fate of a man who had dared to write a truthful book and incurred the wrath of the powers-that-be in some totalitarian country, or discussed the poetry of a Dalit Panther poet, or deplored the banning of a play for its explicit sex. Sagar had liked being part of this stimulating and significant scene. But eventually it began to bore her. It seemed repetitive. Though the actual topics of discussion changed, the attitudes of the speakers were static. It might simply have been the result of their remaining the same while she herself was growing, changing. Whatever the reason, she began to feel that the things her parents talked about, cared about, had no bearing on her life, did not touch her world.

She said now, "Why is the water milky?"

"I think it's because of the sand, but I'm not sure."

Sagar picked up small pebbles and tried to lob them into the stream.

Rohini said, "Do stop fidgeting."

Sagar said, "What's that bird?"

"What bird?" Gautam said.

"The one that's calling. It has a three-note call. Listen. Do you hear it? The middle note is higher. Like this." She mimicked the call.

"I don't know," Gautam said a little ruefully. He thought that Sagar could make him feel inadequate as no one else ever had, by asking some simple but impossible-to-answer question. She was always like this. He was sure that she asked more questions than any other child, and she probably kept a mental tally of all the ones he could not answer. Once when she was quite small she had asked him how long pigeons lived — a question apparently prompted by a conversation about the mess pigeons made on their balcony — and upon his saying that he didn't know, had said exasperatedly, "Daddy, don't you know *anything*?" He was not an ignorant fool, and so he thought that the only reason for these unsatisfactory encounters with his daughter must be that she took a malicious pleasure in showing up the deficiencies in his knowledge.

Chin resting on knees, Sagar moodily watched the stream. The same stream ran by their hut and Rohini complained that its constant din got on her nerves. Gautam said that they had the ocean next to their building in Bombay and that was pretty noisy. She said that was different. The sound varied, it receded and came back, there was a pattern to it. This sound was like something inexorable that you couldn't escape. Gautam had smiled at her fancy.

Sagar liked the sound of the water, and she liked to watch it hurtling over the whitish rocks, to think of the mind-boggling snows that kept melting to fill all these streams and keep them flowing throughout the summer.

A yellow spot at the edge of the water intruded upon her attention and resolved itself into a girl in a yellow dress, apparently washing clothes in the water. Sagar knew it must be one of the hippies. She said, "I'm going down to the stream," and quickly, before anyone could object, started down the hill at a run. For all her bulk she could run quite fast, but there was no grace in her. Her movements gave the impression of excessive expenditure of energy.

Rohini looked at her daughter's back sadly. She had always been an attractive woman, and still retained her youthful figure and looks. She could wear almost anything, and had excellent taste in clothes. People told her she looked like Sagar's older sister and, though she always made deprecating sounds at this remark, it pleased her. She had never thought of herself as having any decorative value. It was just that how she looked and dressed was part of the totality of what she was, of the way she faced life. And Sagar was also a part of it. She had wanted a daughter. At a late age she had suddenly felt an overwhelming need to create someone in her own image, to leave her behind as an enduring mark of her own existence. She had called the girl Sagarika for the sinuous grace of the ocean which was ever visible from their flat. She was disappointed not by Sagar's lack of beauty but by her refusal to care about her appearance. When she was little, Rohini had dressed her in short flared dresses or tights and embroidered tops, and with her black hair cut short and fringed in the front, she had always looked very smart. She was always plump, but as a teenager she became dumpy. Now at nearly twenty she was overweight. She refused to accept any curbs on her diet. She wore faded jeans and T-shirts, and grew her hair to an awkward in-between length and tied it back with a rubber band. Within limits, Rohini admitted, there could be a sort of charm in looking bohemian. But there was nothing charming about the way Sagar looked. She looked merely sloppy and uncared for, and consistently resisted Rohini's attempts to make her wear clothes which would hide rather than accentuate her dumpiness, or teach her the importance of good grooming.

Sagar saw that the girl was indeed washing clothes. She was all yellow. She had on a long yellow dress and her yellow hair lay lankly on her shoulders. She rubbed a piece of clothing against a rock and held it in the stream to rinse it.

Sagar said, "Hello."

The girl looked up and gave a fleeting non-committal smile. Her eyes, though not unfriendly, were totally devoid of warmth or curiosity.

"Isn't the water awfully cold?"

The girl nodded without looking up.

"Where are you from?"

"France."

"How long are you here for?"

"I am not sure."

At least she was not averse to answering questions. Sagar said, seeking to provide, in the way she understood, a frame of reference for the girl, "What does you father do?"

"He is dead."

"And you mother?"

"She too."

"Oh."

Sagar didn't know whether to say she was sorry. The girl's tone was so matter-of-fact that she didn't seem to invite sympathy. In fact she didn't seem to invite any communication at all. Discouraged, Sagar stood and watched. Ever since she had first seen the hippies in the bazaar, she had wanted to talk to one of them. In a group they seemed, in their colourful maxis, lungis, togas, pajamas, rather like a flock of exotic-plumed birds. The girl paid no attention to her at all, and Sagar began to feel angry at the rebuff, the more so because the girl looked so delicate and vulnerable. She heard Rohini call, "Come on, Sagar, we'd better start back, it's getting late."

The trim woman in dark pink pants and black turtleneck seemed suddenly like a stranger to Sagar. She experienced a swift fantasy in which a fat middle-aged woman with graying untidy hair was shouting and waving her arms wildly and she herself was shouting, "I'm coming, what's all the fuss about?"

Rohini said, "Were you *talking* to the girl?"

"No, just watching her."

"She must be mad washing in that ice-cold water."

"Where else can she wash? She probably doesn't even have running cold water where she lives. Some of them live in real shacks, or camp out."

"Whose fault is that? Nobody asked them to come here and live in poverty."

"They *are* a dirty, unkempt lot," Gautam said. "I can't understand why we allow them into the country."

"Why shouldn't we?" Sagar said. "They don't do anybody any harm."

"They don't do anyone any good either," Rohini said.

"Why does everyone have to do any good? What's wrong with living your own life without hurting anyone?"

Gautam said, "But they do harm others, by spreading the use of drugs."

"Indians knew about using drugs before the hippie generation was born," Sagar said.

"Maybe, but drug use in India was quite different. Drugs were not very widely used, and they were not used as an escape from the responsibilities of normal life. And most important of all, drug use was not fashionable. The hippies have made it into a cult."

"Still, they don't coerce anyone into using drugs, do they?"

"Not directly. But indirectly they do, by setting up a model which others want to follow. Also, their taking drugs has a demoralizing influence on any society where they live, because it encourages illicit traffic and leads to all sorts of criminal activity."

"That's because of the outdated laws. There wouldn't be illicit traffic if there weren't laws against possessing and selling drugs."

"You don't know what you are talking about, Sagar. You are just spouting the jargon of your generation without understanding the deeper social and psychological forces at work behind a social phenomenon. Force or coercion doesn't have to be only the direct and obvious kind that can be fought openly."

Rohini said, before Sagar could say anything, "All that apart, I think they are an insult to the countryside. They are ragged and filthy, they sleep anywhere, cook anywhere, defecate anywhere."

"That's the way many Indians live too," Sagar said.

"They are different."

"How?"

"They have a sense of personal dignity which the hippies completely lack. And since they belong here, they don't behave in the irresponsible manner of the hippies."

"I don't see how the hippies are irresponsible."

"If you refuse to see the obvious, Sagar, nobody can make you."

The argument was abruptly cut short because of a rain shower. Although there had been clouds, the rain had not seemed imminent. There had been no sudden darkening, no thunder, no warning that the sky was going to open up.

Rohini said, "Hurry up, Sagar, don't drag your feet."

"We're going to be drenched even if we run." Sagar continued walking at her normal pace, enjoying the violence of the rain.

As she opened the front door she heard her father's voice, "Come now, it started long before that." Rohini said, "But it wasn't so bad. She wasn't so completely antagonistic. I think I can definitely trace it to the episode with the boy. We should never have sent her to the camp."

Her next words were drowned in a paroxysm of sneezing.

## 5

Gautam had said, "Why not let her go? She is so apathetic about most things, I think her being so keen on it is sufficient reason to send her."

"She's keen on it only because it's the fashionable thing to do this summer."

"What difference does that make? Young people always have fads. I can't understand why you are so dead set against it."

"I wouldn't be if it was something worthwhile. But you know and I know it's just a stunt. What can these children accomplish in two weeks of living in a village? What possible good can it do either to them or to the villagers?"

She was outraged, both because Gautam had seen fit to interfere when up until now he had left all decisions concerning Sagar entirely up to her, and because he refused to see the sense in her position. In the end Sagar had gone to the camp.

It was a village near Panvel, set partly into the side of a hill, picturesque, but riddled with poverty and sickness and dirt. They lived in the village school dormitory style, girls in one room, boys in another. They had the most primitive bathing arrangements, having to be content with pouring a bucket of cold water over themselves while still half-dressed, behind an inadequately rigged shelter of gunnybags through holes in which the bather could often see a child's curious eye peeking. They cooked sketchy meals on chulas made by arranging three large stones, and they had to scrounge around the countryside for sticks to burn in the chulas. And whatever water they needed had to be brought by the bucket from a well near by.

They assigned themselves the job of making a wider and more nearly all-weather road out of the cart track which became so muddy in the monsoon that it was impassable. They worked all day and at night sat around a camp fire, chatted with the villagers and played word games. Sagar was realistic enough to admit that she wouldn't like to live in this style for very long, but it was fun while it lasted. She enjoyed the stimulation of doing something different, and the camaraderie which develops in an informal group of this sort. There was also the deeper and more complex appreciation of the whole new world which the camp opened up for her. And, of course, her meeting with Nitin. The small dark boy with his fiery hurtful tongue had drawn her strangely. He talked about himself with an almost aggressive frankness. His father worked in a cloth mill, his mother was illiterate, and he was the fourth of six children who barely had breathing space in a two-room tenement. Sagar was reluctant to give information about herself, but he prised it out of her and then used it to torment her. "What motivates a girl like you to come to a camp like this? Is it a new kind of kick?" She didn't answer such questions because she could not use words as facilely as he did, and in his presence she felt ashamed of her wealth, could find nothing to say in justification of it. He seemed to take pleasure in tormenting her, but finally was touched by her willingness to submit herself to the punishment. She never saw him as really cruel. She admired the ease and real concern he displayed in dealing with the villagers. He could squat unconcernedly in their huts on the mud or cowdung floor and talk to them over the dark oversweet cup of tea they offered him. Once she saw him pick up, without any apparent hesitation, a filthy, snot-nosed child who had fallen down and grazed his knees, dust his clothes off, wipe his eyes and nose on his own handkerchief and comfort him, all the while watching her with a mocking smile as if daring her to do the same.

She followed him about with doglike devotion and worked extra hard at any chore that was assigned to her, just to earn his respect. When she finally sensed his resistance weaken, and felt that he cared a little for her, she almost could not believe

28

it. Once when they were by themselves, she shyly referred to her physical unattractiveness, and he said, contemptuously dismissing this very important aspect of her life, "Why waste time worrying about inessentials?" Then he added, "Don't knock yourself. The secret of success and happiness is that you must always believe in yourself. If you can't believe in yourself, there's nothing else left to believe in." Sagar suddenly glimpsed vulnerability behind his tough exterior, and was touched by his unintended expression of it.

When she returned to Bombay, Rohini sensed the change in her, and attributed it rightly to a romantic involvement. Sagar was secretive, but Rohini, through adroit questioning, learned enough to alarm her. She asked Sagar to bring Nitin home and although Sagar did not like the idea, it was a reasonable request and she could not very well refuse. Of course she was not at all sure that Nitin would agree to come, but he did.

The first time he came, Rohini showed very little interest, was even a little remote. There were several visits and she gradually became friendly, gracious, charming. Expecting a wall of resistance and meeting none, Nitin was confused, exposing his inadequacy in Sagar's natural environment, his utter lack of social poise. Sagar did not mind this. She would not have minded it if he had been taunting and insolent, if he had flaunted his poverty aggressively, or even if he had been sullen and uncommunicative. What she could not accept was a Nitin reduced to stuttering shyness, refusing to meet her mother's eye, making, thinking it was necessary to make, inane polite conversation and failing at it, slinking away full of his own inferiority and then taking his anger out on Sagar, trying to hurt her viciously.

Finally Sagar had no heart left for fighting with him. She allowed their relationship to fizzle out. He said bitterly that she had cooled off because she found that he could not after all measure up to her wealth and social position. She countered his allegation only with a sad smile, refusing to be goaded into denying it because in one way it was true. She felt a certain inevitability about what had happened, yet she also felt that her mother had somehow manipulated the events to ensure this outcome.

She missed Nitin, the stimulation of being with him, the delight of being able to share everything with someone, of being totally herself without self-consciousness. She spent hours imagining elaborate scenes of reunion but even while she imagined them, she knew they rang false. What her mother had destroyed could not be put back together. Sometimes she thought that it would not have been so bad if she and Rohini had talked, argued, fought about it. But that was not Rohini's way. She was, as Nitin sarcastically said, civilized. She did not deal directly with unpleasant matters.

Once, when Sagar was about eight, Rohini had walked in on her and her friends playing under her bed in a closed and darkened room. They had been "exploring" one another and it must have been obvious to Rohini from their flushed and guilty expressions. After the other children had left she asked Sagar, "What were you doing under the bed?"

"Playing ghosts."

"In the dark?"

"Of course. It's more scary."

"It's not nice playing under the bed like that."

"Why?" Sagar said, almost goading her.

"You had the curtains pulled, the door closed, the bedspread pulled down, and so many of you crammed in under the bed. You could have suffocated. Promise me you will never do that again."

Sagar waited but Rohini had said all she was going to say. Sagar felt relieved at getting off so lightly, but a part of her wished that Mummy would confront her with the truth and punish her. In the long run the continuing feeling of guilt was more hurtful than a spanking would have been.

In the same way, Rohini not only desisted from ever referring to Nitin, she behaved as though nothing out of the ordinary had happened. This was what Sagar found most difficult to take. She wanted her mother to acknowledge, by some gesture, the fact that she, Sagar, was undergoing a profound emotional crisis.

Rohini congratulated herself for handling a difficult situation with tact and delicacy instead of forcing a confrontation. Simply by taking a relationship out of one context and into another, she succeeded in proving to Sagar its complete untenability. She was happy that Sagar was perceptive enough to see it and break off with the boy. She was also relieved that Sagar took the whole thing more or less in her stride and did not seem exactly heartbroken.

## 6

Sagar felt as though she was bursting out of her skin with a sense of release. Rohini had a bad cold and they had had quite a conversation about it at breakfast.

Gautam said, "You must have caught it yesterday. That rain was cold."

Rohini said, "I suppose we should have carried an umbrella. But it didn't even look like rain when we started out."

She said this in a slightly aggrieved tone as though she felt that somebody should have warned her of the unpredictability of the weather.

She sneezed again and Gautam felt her forehead and said, "You've got a temperature. You'd better get back into bed." She got back into bed and Gautam insisted, despite protests, on staying with her in case she needed anything.

Sagar thought it disgusting that anyone should let themselves be babied in this way over a silly cold, but she was happy to be free of her parents' company. It felt so good to be on her own to explore the place that she felt like running, jumping, dancing.

She went for a long walk, exploring paths where she had not been before, crossing over to the Leh road and walking a few miles along it, feeling thrilled at walking on the highest road in the world, as the sign said. There were people working on the road, and they stared at her, but when she smiled, they smiled back. The women were readier to smile, the men on the whole more taciturn, measuring her with their eyes consideringly. The children played in the dust by the road, and the stream flowed boisterously in the background.

When the sun began to get hot and she was tired, she made her way to the bazaar. She saw the hippies as usual clustered around the bazaar, lending a kind of mad colour to the otherwise drab gray street. She wondered if perhaps she could manage to get into a conversation with one of them, but they seemed to move in groups. Finally in a tea shop where she went to get a snack, she saw one sitting by himself. She went over to his table and said, "May I join you?" She hoped that he knew English.

He looked up, startled, then smiled and said, "Sure," without enthusiasm but also without hesitation.

"My name's Sagar."

"Tony."

"Where are you from, Tony?"

"U.S.A."

"How long have you been here?"

"Month or so."

"How did you happen to come here?"

"I don't know. I was with a group, we were travelling in Europe, the Middle East. Someone said why not go to India, so we came."

32

He had dirty blond hair and a beard, and deep blue eyes. He wore cream-coloured pajamas and a dull red-and-black kurta with a batik print.

She said, "Do you like it here?" and immediately felt that it was rather pointless asking him this question which one normally asks foreigners. It didn't seem applicable.

He said, "Sure." His voice was non-committal.

"Are you here for just a short while or do you plan to stay long?"

He shrugged. "I don't know."

"What did you do before you came here?"

"I was in college."

"You left college to travel around?"

"That's right."

"Why?"

"I don't know. I couldn't understand what it was all about. At one point I asked myself if I wanted to be like my father, like thousands of men like him, and the answer came no, so I left."

"Just like that? Did they give you permission to go?"

Suddenly he laughed. "Permission? I told them I was going. That was it."

Sagar felt like a fool. For a while she concentrated on eating. She had ordered *chhole* and *bhature* and they were delicious. She had often seen the enormous dishes of *chhole* garnished with raw onions, wedges of lemon and green coriander, and felt her mouth water. But Rohini and Gautam thought these places too dirty to patronize. She sipped her cardamom-flavoured tea, trying not to scald her mouth and hand on the hot glass in which they served tea instead of in a cup and saucer.

When they left the tea-shop she said, "Do you mind if I walk with you?"

"No."

They walked some way into the woods and then Tony decided to sit down. She said, picking up the thread of their earlier conversation, "What exactly do you object to in your parents' life?"

"Everything. They go after all the wrong things, things that don't matter."

"What, for instance?"

"Oh, money, possessions, status. And they are always running so hard after what they don't have, they forget to enjoy what they have. This whole idea is cockeyed. You value success most, which means you value people only for their ability to succeed, which mostly means making money. At the same time you hate and fear them, because you see them as threats. You stand continuously in competition with everyone else, and you find you can't afford to trust anyone. By the same rules you are valued only for your ability to make money, but you can't accept this. You want people to love you for yourself. Your life becomes full of contradictions and you end up feeling frustrated, miserable, full of hate and fear instead of the love and happiness which you thought you were aiming at."

"You don't think one should have any ambition, then?"

"Not if it distorts your judgement, deprives you of sleep and gives you ulcers."

"It also gives you motivation, initiative. It can bring out the best in you."

"Also the worst."

Sagar was not as adroit as he was at arguing. He had probably thought it all out carefully, while she was using on-the-spot arguments. But there was stimulation in being with him, talking to him, the same kind of stimulation that was there in being with Nitin, although they were very different. Nitin was consumed with ambition, determined to overcome the disadvantages he was born with, to prove he was as good as anyone else. Tony had dissociated himself from the world which accepted such aspirations as valid.

She said, "But you must want to do something with your life."

"Why? I take life as it comes. I don't feel I have to plan everything at the start. If you know exactly what you are going to be doing ten years from now, there's no room for surprises. You rule out the possibility of anything new, exciting."

Sagar felt as if she was looking at things from the other end. The acceptance of the idea that life did not have to be forced into a rigid frame, or planned for with any great foresight, but could be lived simply by meeting whatever exigencies arose, was suddenly presented to her as a possibility.

She said, "What do you do for money? You must still need money to live on."

"I try to earn it when necessary. I find work for a few days. Sometimes one of the other kids has money. If we all run out I write and ask my Dad to send me some."

"You reject everything he stands for, but you accept his money!"

"That's the whole point. He belongs to the system. I don't. I don't think money creates an obligation."

"What if he refuses to send you any?"

"That will be okay too. I'll manage." He laughed. "But he won't refuse. He is too afraid that I might step outside the law to get money. He keeps me in funds to save himself trouble, dishonour, guilt."

Sagar was a little shaken that this soft-spoken, gentle-seeming man could be ruthless enough to exploit his father's weaknesses. Yet she saw an irrefutable logic in his position. If you did not accept money as a value at all, the rest of it followed. But was it possible to sustain such a position? While most of the world considered the earning and possession of money as the core of human endeavour and the basis of social hierarchy, could the remaining few get by with considering money as simply a thing, necessary only in so far as it supported life, but unimportant in itself, so that the possession of it does not confer superiority, and the giving and taking of it does not create obligation?

The long walk of the morning and her full stomach and the coolness of the woods made her drowsy. She lay down beside him and closed her eyes. Just as she was drifting off to sleep she heard the bird.

"Tony!"

"Um?"

"What's that bird? The one that just called? Listen, there he is again."

She was trying to locate him, as usual unsuccessfully. She wondered how bird watchers ever saw anything other than crows.

"I don't know," Tony said without interest.

Disappointed, Sagar closed her eyes again. She did not know how much later it was when she awoke, looked beside her and saw Tony miraculously still there. The shadows of the trees were lengthening and good sense told her that she ought to go home. But she was reluctant to let go of Tony and perhaps never see him again.

Then he was awake too. He showed neither surprise nor pleasure at her continuing presence. She was simply there, and he accepted her for the time being as he accepted the trees and the grass and the gathering darkness.

She said, "Where do you live?"

"In a house up there."

"Up where?"

"Beyond the log huts."

She remembered seeing a rather dilapidated old house there.

"Do you pay rent?"

"Yeah. A lot of us live there, and one of us pays."

"Can anyone come and stay there? Can I?"

"Sure, if you bring your own sleeping bag."

She got up. "It's getting late. I've got to go. What's it called, the house where you live?"

"Mountainview."

"It's been nice meeting you, Tony. I hope I'll see you again."

"Sure," he said non-committally.

As she walked back, she felt dispirited. It occurred to her that after spending hours together, they had not achieved any communication. He had been willing enough to answer questions, even eloquent in his answers, but had asked none, displayed no curiosity about her at all. Well, she told herself with only a little self-pity, I imposed myself on him without invitation, so I have no right to complain.


7


"Don't stand in the open door. You've got a cold," Gautam said. He sounded peevish. Rohini thought, as though it was not the possibility of my getting sick that bothered him, but the trouble it would mean to him. The thought frightened her. Was she imagining things or had everything really changed?

Gautam said more gently, "Please come in, Rohini. If you want, I'll go and look for her."

She said dully, "If I want. Don't you feel anything about her, Gautam? You never have, have you?"

"Have you?" he said, so softly that at first the words didn't register. Then they suddenly made an explosion inside her.

"Of course I have."

"There's no of course about it, Ro." He went quickly out of the door before she had a chance to say anything. He returned about half an hour later, reporting that a shopkeeper remembered seeing Sagar. She had eaten there and left with a hippie early in the afternoon. But now she was nowhere in the bazaar.

37

Rohini said, "I just knew it had to be a man. There couldn't be anything else that kept her all this time."

"How can you say that?"

"Well, you have proof of it, don't you? Gautam, if you weren't so blind, you would see how she plays up to a man, any man. Even people like shop assistants and lift boys are not beneath her attention. You saw the way she carried on in the taxi that day. She even carries on a ridiculously romantic correspondence with a pen-friend in England whom she has never met."

Gautam was speechless. He wanted to ask her how she knew about Sagar's correspondence, but realized that it could only be through opening her letters. Somehow this discovery affected him more than anything Rohini had said about Sagar.

When Sagar finally came in, Rohini demanded, "Where were you?"

"In the morning I went for a walk, then I had a late lunch in the bazaar, and since then I've been walking around in the woods," Sagar said as though reciting something she had learned by heart.

"All by yourself?"

"Yes."

"Don't lie, Sagar. Someone in the bazaar saw you with a hippie."

"What do you do, spy on me?"

"If you behave irresponsibly, you deserve to be spied on. Where did you pick him up?"

"I met him in the tea-shop where I had lunch."

"Did he come and start talking to you?"

Sagar would have liked to say yes but she was afraid she might get Tony in trouble. She knew from a conversation Gautam had had with the tourist officer that at best, the authorities only tolerated the hippies. If they could find a reason to throw someone out, they would gladly do so.

She said, "No, he was sitting by himself when I went in. All the other tables were full so I asked him if I could share his."

"I see," Rohini said slowly and deliberately. "And then you spent the rest of the day with him."

Sagar did not say anything.

Suddenly Rohini blazed, "What kind of a girl are you that you can't keep away from men? Are you so sex-crazy that you have to pick up scum?"

Sagar burst into tears. "He is not like that. Just because he's a hippie, you've no right to call him names. He is a nice person."

Rohini gave a short ugly laugh. "Nice person! He would as soon rob you or rape you as talk to you."

Sagar was weeping hysterically now. "That's not true," she said. "All we did was talk. He didn't even touch me."

"Do you expect me to believe that?"

Gautam said, "Leave her alone, Rohini."

"You should at least invent lies that are believable."

"I said that's enough," Gautam said. "Let the poor child eat dinner."

"I'm not hungry," Sagar cried and ran into her bedroom, slamming and locking the door after her.

"Child! I suppose like all fathers you have this cherished image of their daughters as innocent little girls."

"Shut up." Gautam's voice was like a whip-crack and Rohini winced as though he had hit her. She shook her head as if to clear it and said, "I'm sorry."

Gautam went to the kitchen and heated the soup they had had for dinner. He filled a bowl with it and knocked on Sagar's door.

"Sagar, open the door. I've brought you some hot soup."

There was no answer.

"Sagar, please open the door. You shouldn't go to bed on an empty stomach."

He waited but there was no answer, and no movement that he could detect. Finally he thought she must be asleep. He tried to visualise her sleeping and saw the childhood Sagar, the curve of a sleep-flushed cheek above the covers, tousled hair on the pillow, small full mouth slack. He remembered a large nondescript stuffed animal which she had loved to take to bed with her. Rohini had finally thrown it away because it had become filthy and could not be washed. Sagar had been heartbroken and had refused to accept a substitute and so had learned to sleep without her stuffed companion.

Gautam unexpectedly felt a wave of protective tenderness for this child, his child. He wanted to envelop her with love and keep her from ever getting hurt.


8


It was early, just beginning to be light. Gautam stood outside the hut and smoked a cigarette — something he rarely did so early in the morning. It didn't even taste good but he felt some such action was necessary to keep him in touch with the known and the normal. The beauty of the washed new day — there had been another rainstorm during the night — was powerless to dissipate the tired and depressed feeling with which he had fallen asleep and, just four hours later, come awake.

Last night when he went to his bedroom Rohini was crying.

"What are *you* crying about?"

"I said I am sorry, Gautam. Don't be unkind. I don't know what got into me."

Without answering he turned away and started getting ready for bed. He had every intention of ignoring her tears but finally was moved to pity by the unabating storm. He stood over her and said, "Don't, Rohini."

Suddenly she pulled him to her and clung to him, asking, begging him to make love to her.

He said, "But I thought you were bleeding."

"Just a little. It doesn't matter."

He thought, it matters to me. But she had swept him with her on a tide which was not love, or tenderness, or any emotion he had experienced before. The revulsion he had felt afterwards was still very much with him. He felt used, wrung out, by this furious physical joining. Rohini seemed to be at peace afterwards, and her sleep this morning when he slipped out had been deep and untroubled.

A bird called, Sagar's bird, and he smiled a little sadly and thought that before they left this place he must identify the bird for her.

Rohini said behind him, "Would you like some coffee, Gautam?"

Her voice was hesitant, even shy, like a young girl's when she is not sure of her reception. But across the dining table he saw that her face looked ravaged, far from fresh and young. He felt sorry for her. Having made perfection her habitual milieu, she was finding it impossible to face imperfection in herself.

She said, "Gautam, let's go back."

"Go back?"

"Home, I mean. To Bombay."

"So soon?"

"There's something about this place, it frightens me. I feel my life going out of control. I don't want to stay here any longer."

"Don't be fanciful, darling."

"You can call it fanciful or anything you like. I don't care. I just want to leave."

"But we planned to stay two weeks. We can't just cut a holiday short for no good reason." Incongruously, he thought of their friends in Bombay. "What, back so soon?" What would they answer? We didn't like it there? We got bored?

Rohini said, "There is a good reason."

"What about Sagar? She'll be awfully disappointed."

"It can't be helped."

Gautam sighed and poured himself another cup. The cigarette had made his throat raw and the coffee tasted awful, but the simple familiar act of drinking it gave him comfort. He was thinking of how reluctant Sagar had been to come on this trip. They had never taken her travelling with them, thinking that she would be happiest and most secure in her own familiar surroundings rather than being carted all over the countryside and exposed to bad food, impure water and all sorts of infections. Somehow, the habit had continued even after Sagar grew up, so that now she was surprised when she found that she was included in their holiday plans. Rohini had felt that the holiday might ease the tensions between them, by taking them away from situations which were full of possibilities for conflict. Sagar was doubtful, but Rohini had been very persuasive. Finally it was the attraction of seeing the Himalayan countryside that had persuaded Sagar. She seemed to be enjoying the holiday, and Gautam thought that it would be unfair to suddenly announce that they were going back because they had had enough, without even consulting her.

He said, "Perhaps it is wrong to have children late in life."

Rohini's face was impassive. She seemed turned inwards. Anyway, he was not sure what he was trying to say, so there was no point in getting through to her. He continued to sip his coffee. The second cup tasted better than the first, and he felt unexpectedly hungry for a good large breakfast. He imagined the three of them sitting down to a breakfast of eggs and sausages, bread and butter and jam, and plenty of coffee, talking companionably while they ate, enjoying the view of the deodar forest with the primitive little temple showing through the trees.

He said, "I'll see if Sagar is stirring yet."
But before he reached her room something that had nudged
his consciousness earlier, suddenly assumed significance. The
front door had not been bolted when he opened it in the
morning. He felt almost no surprise when he saw that Sagar's
room was empty.

9

Sagar sat up, feeling dazed and confused. In the cold light of
day what she had done seemed melodramatic. She felt that if
she had given herself time to think until morning she would
probably not have had the courage to sneak out of the house.
She tried to reconstruct last night's scene and realized that
what had upset her so badly was not so much being
condemned without a hearing, being called practically a
nymphomaniac, but the image of her mother shouting and
snarling and stooping to calling her that. It was as if a known
dimension of her life had suddenly changed out of
recognition. Thinking about it now brought a smile to her
lips. "At least," she thought, "there was something honest
about her, for a change. She said exactly what she meant to
say. When people are honest, you at least know what they really
think of you, where you stand."
Tony brought her a glass of coffee, strong and bitter and
black and tasting of smoke. She didn't like it, but sipped it
anyway, feeling the hot liquid warming her, and becoming
suddenly aware of hunger.
"What do you do for food?" she asked him.
"Sometimes we cook something here, but more often we eat at
a *dhaba* which has very inexpensive food."

She had not changed the night before, and there was still some money in her pocket. That was lucky, she thought. She did not think about what she would do when she went through the money. Without putting it in so many words, she took it that somehow she would be back with her parents.

She had a perfunctory wash at a stream. She had not had a bath the day before and felt dirty, but she knew she could and would stay without a bath for a week if this ice-cold stream was the only water available for bathing. She wouldn't wash clothes either. It amused her to think how quickly ideas and attitudes could change to fit a new context.

The *dhaba* was a dingy wooden shack where they served beans and puris and tea and were not too particular about cleanliness. She looked round at her breakfast companions, products of an affluent society, choosing to live in primitive conditions, eating a cheap unvarying diet without worrying about its nutritional value or the unhygienic surroundings in which it was cooked and served. What were they doing? What were they looking for which was worth subjecting themselves to these deprivations?

They did not question her presence. They did not talk to her, but they accepted her. She thought, how nice to simply go among new people and be accepted without introducing yourself. And yet their lack of curiosity piqued her. At first she thought they were wary because she was an outsider and an Indian. Then she observed that they behaved the same way with one another. Even when they conversed with one another, each talked only about himself. Information was freely offered without being sought. This really amounted to everyone carrying on a conversation with himself. She heard one man narrating his experiences as a taxi driver in New York. It was actually quite an amusing monologue, but the girl to whom it was addressed only smiled and nodded absently. When he stopped, she launched into a monologue about her life with a divorced mother who had a succession of lovers.

44

Perhaps we are all like that, Sagar thought. Nobody is really interested in anybody but himself. Only, people who live in a more conventional world make believe it's not so. The hippies don't waste time in pretence.

In the late afternoon finally Gautam came. She was beginning to wonder whether they would come after her at all, and if they didn't what she would do.

He said, "Sagar, what are you doing here?"

"I am living here."

"You felt you could walk out and not bother even to leave a note telling us where you had gone?" He was angry, but his anger was tightly controlled, his voice formal.

"Your mother has been worried sick about you."

"I didn't think Mummie would care."

"My God, Sagar! Do you know what you're saying?"

He stared at her and she stared back, defying him to deny the truth of what she was saying, almost willing him to do it. But he turned his eyes away, looking suddenly defeated, and said, "Aren't you coming back?" He sounded almost as though he expected her to say no, in fact would be quite relieved if she did.

"No," she said.

"Rohini wants to go back."

"So go back."

"What about you?" he said unhappily. She felt an impersonal kind of pity for him, because he didn't seem to know how to handle this.

She said, "I'll manage. Don't worry about me."

"When will you come back?"

"I don't know."

"All right, Sagar." He took his wallet from his pocket. "Here's some money. I'll leave more with the tourist officer. There will be enough for your fare also. I don't think it's safe for you to have too much money on you."

He sounded brisker now, as though relieved that this difficult meeting was coming to an end.

"Would you like me to bring your clothes here?"

"No, I don't want all of them. Just a couple of changes. You can leave that at the tourist office too."

"All right. And Sagar. . . . "

For a moment his face softened. She thought he was about to put his arms around her, hug her close.

"Yes, Daddy."

"Take care," he merely said.

"I will."

She stood looking at him till he disappeared. A few minutes later Tony came by. "Why are you crying, kid?" he said, "Why didn't you go back with him?"

"I guess because he didn't really want me to," she said.

## 10

"I wish you'd go and talk to her," Gautam said. "I just didn't seem to be able to get through to her."

"What makes you think I'll fare better?" Rohini was putting a lot of angry energy into packing.

"You've always been closer to her."

"Gautam, I'm simply not going to that hippies' den to talk to her. She didn't so much as inform me when she walked out of here. Why should I waste my time trying to persuade her to come back? She'll be back when she's had enough of the new thrill. Or when she runs out of money. She can't have very much with her."

"I gave her some."

"What? Why on earth did you do that?"

"You don't *want* her to starve, do you? Besides, I don't think it would have made any difference if I hadn't given her money."

"A hungry stomach can be a powerful force."

"It wouldn't have been fair."

"Fair! Would you say what she has done is fair to me?"

"Parents can't use the same weapons that a child uses."

"Yes, and the child counts on it and blackmails the parents. Well, this once I refuse to submit myself to blackmail."

Gautam watched her silently for a while. Finally he said, "You really won't change your mind about going to see her?"

"No."

"Something might happen to her."

"Whose fault will that be? I am sorry, Gautam, but I can't see myself forever trying to protect her from the consequences of her rash actions."

# 11

Sagar could not sleep much that night. Several times she almost got up and started walking. But an obstinate pride kept her from it. If she went back now, uninvited, she could never have any self-respect again. She kept hoping that when they left in the morning her parents would come by and insist that she stop this nonsense and get into the taxi. In the end, tired, she fell asleep long after midnight, and slept until late, waking with the thought that they had left without her after all. She went to a spot from where she could see the front door of the hut. She saw it locked.

She spent most of the day alone, walking around aimlessly, eating when she felt like it, finding after all that she was enjoying the freedom, the feeling of not being accountable to anyone but herself. She wondered if this was what being grown up meant. She stopped at the tourist office to collect her bag and money. The tourist officer, a good-looking young man dressed immaculately in a terylene suit and tie and well-shined stylish shoes, told her that she could continue living in the hut as they had reserved it for a month and occupied it for a little less than two weeks. On an impulse she took the key from him and went to the hut. She had a long hot shower and changed and washed her clothes, and then returned to Mountainview, still carrying the key and feeling like a traitor. The next day she returned the key, telling the tourist officer that she didn't want to live in the hut and he could rent it to someone else. She asked him if she could keep the blankets she had taken. He considered this — anything outside the rules required careful consideration — and told her with a pleasant smile that she could keep them, so long as she returned them in the condition they were in when she left. He also told that she could come to him if she needed any help. He had probably been given some idea of the situation by her father. He was quite nice, but in his own way just as impersonal as Tony. He must be like this with all the tourists. That was his job. Therefore, his polite interest was an obstruction to communication rather than an aid to it.

She went back to Mountainview and found that Tony was not there. Feeling rather lost without him, she went looking for him and found him finally at the post office. She invited him to lunch and found a whole group materializing around her. She thought that these people had the cunning of those who lived on the fringe of society. They could smell money and didn't mind sponging. But they also had the generosity that such people usually have. They quite willingly shared with others whatever little they had, without any thought about saving it for tomorrow.

Gradually she got to know some of the others in the group and began to feel more at ease with them. She spent a great deal of time observing them, wondering what made them tick.

There was a man called David who specially intrigued her. He sat most of the day under a tree outside the house and stared straight ahead with glazed eyes. He was a big man, thin to the point of emaciation, so that his bones seemed to hang loosely without a coordinating frame. He wore a dirty lungi and a torn shirt with LOVE printed across the chest. The dark stubble on his face made the skin surrounding it look startlingly white. A woman in a long shapeless dress was always with him, sometimes kneeling behind him to comb and braid his long hair, sometimes urging food on him, trying to feed him with a spoon, sometimes just sitting with him. A little boy, naked below the waist, usually sat near her sucking his thumb.

David lived in a world of his own, totally unresponsive to those around him, even to the woman and child. Sagar thought that the word love, which was a communion between two people, was probably the most inappropriate that he could have found to display on his chest. Such a feeling could not exist in his emotional repertoire. She wondered how the woman could feel any tenderness for a man turned totally inward under the influence of some drug. She herself found him a little frightening, if not repulsive.

She asked the woman one day if the little boy was her son.

"Yes."

"How old is he?"

"Five."

"Aren't you going to put him in school or anything?"

"I haven't really thought about it."

The boy seemed pathetic to Sagar, he looked so forlorn and uncared for. She tried to make friends with him. His mother did not object to it. She didn't seem to care with whom he was and he often attached himself to one of the others when they

49

went out, resuming his place by his mother when she returned. There were two other children in the group, and they also got handed into the care of whoever had the time or inclination to look after them. In the fashion of the joint family, Sagar thought. But she immediately corrected herself. No, it wasn't like a joint family at all, which had a definite structure, and clearly defined and unchangeable relationships. Here there was nothing a child could count on except the presence of someone who could look after its physical needs for the time being.

She said to Tony, "How can these children have any sense of security?"

"Why not? I'm sure they are as secure as any other children."

"It's different when children belong to a proper family."

"What do you mean by a proper family? Do you think it is possible to live happily under only one system?"

"No, of course not. Even now many systems do exist, but they are all based on some kind of fairly permanent nucleus."

"They don't have to be."

"Maybe not."

He smiled. "You don't really want to admit that a very different kind of system can exist which is based on a broader concept of love rather than the narrow possessive and selfish love which the standard unit family sponsors."

Love. That word was always bandied about like a symbol. It sounded almost like too much protesting, a pathetic attempt of these people to convince themselves that they were surrounded by love. Could they, who rejected even a semi-permanent relationship with anyone, who seemed too self-involved to feel even superficial curiosity about others, understand what love was? Then she thought, maybe even our concepts of love are so different that I can't begin to understand theirs. I am so conditioned by the ideas I have absorbed from childhood that I can't make room in my mind for anything that doesn't fit in with them. Maybe love as I know it is a binding, crippling emotion, when it should be a freeing one. Maybe, when you broaden your concept of love to include a great number of people, you become incapable of channelling it into more personal, petty relationships. Like the saints. Are these people close to saints?

She said, "Very few people are capable of such a broad all-enveloping love. Most of us need the security of what you call narrow and possessive love."

"A false feeling of security. Don't you see that it all goes together? If people can be taught to rethink their whole structure of ideas about love and family and the feeling of security —"

"Is that what you have done? Rethink all your ideas and arrange your life accordingly?"

Again he smiled. "By no means. I am just groping, but I know I want something different from what I have had. I want to be freer, and happier. Not bound tight by a system which demands everything from us, sucks us dry of everything that is worthwhile in us, and gives us nothing in return."

"What about the children?"

"What about them?"

"What happens to them?"

"The same thing that happens to other children. They grow up."

"To what sort of life?"

"Any sort of life they want. They are free to choose."

In effect though, Sagar thought, they would not be free to choose. Tony had been able to repudiate his background, but his child would not be able to fit into the other world because it would not be equipped for it. You can give up something you have, you cannot acquire overnight something you don't have. Yet she had to concede that if you believed in a certain way of life, you could not but impose it upon your children. Then did it mean that you fled one prison only to build another kind of prison around yourself, and worse, around your children?

The alternative was wanting your children to have a different sort of life from yours. Like the Kulvis of this valley. They were largely illiterate, and worked as labourers in the fields, on road construction, in the logging camps. Some probably made their living off the tourists. They seemed quite happy. They sang as they worked, smiled at you if you showed any interest in them, went about their work in a matter-of-fact manner. If they were poor and deprived, they did not invite pity. Their needs were few and easily met. They repeated a well-worn pattern of life without question or rebellion.

Yet they were helping to break the pattern by sending their children to school. Sagar had often passed by the school and seen the moon-faced, slant-eyed children sitting solemnly, their round cheeks so raw with the cold that they looked as though someone had put too much rouge on them inexpertly. She had seen a very stern-looking master trying to command the wandering attention of his young charges, helping them to take the first step in the long process of their awakening to the world of learning. Why were the parents helping the children diverge from the pattern they themselves had followed? Certainly not because they thought it was wrong. Why then? Because they were so poor that they felt that a change, any change, had to be for the better? Perhaps they were simply sending their children to school because the government required it. Still, they must be aware that for many of the children, this meant taking steps which could not be retraced. And then, would the children's children or grandchildren perhaps, weary of the burdens this change imposed on them, want to go back to the simplicity and primitivity of their ancestors' lives? Was that what the hippies were trying to do?

## 12

Standing in front of the sparsely stocked news-stand in the bazaar, Sagar noticed the date on a newspaper. She thought, only two weeks to college opening day. So what, she asked herself. Why should it mean anything? College has never interested me very much. Why don't I give it up? Then she thought, but it's my last year. If I give up now I will have wasted all those years of studying. So what, she asked herself again, and walked away from the news-stand, remembering the argument she had had with her mother.

"I don't want to go on with college."

"Why?"

"I'm bored with it. I'd like to do something else."

"What, for instance?"

"Learn typing, take a secretarial course maybe."

"What's the point in that, unless you are going to take a job as a secretary?"

"That's what I was thinking of doing."

"Sagar, you're out of your mind. You've got every opportunity for education. You can do anything. You don't have to work for a living. And you want to take a job as a secretary?"

"Why not?"

Sagar had sulked, and finally Rohini had surrendered conditionally. "All right. I agree that you should do what you want to. But first you have to finish your B.A., then you can do what you want."

Unexpectedly, Sagar felt a little homesick. She wondered whether her mother was thinking of her, worrying about her. Probably not, she thought. Probably she is glad to be rid of me. I was always in the way. I wonder why ever she had me. An accident? But accidents didn't happen to Rohini. Sagar felt angry tears pricking at her eyes and blinked them away. She felt like picking a fight with someone. She bought a bar of chocolate and, still thinking of her mother (Sagar, you've got to think of your weight, don't eat such junk) and munching on the chocolate, she went looking for Tony.

"Tony, do you ever feel homesick?"

"No. I think of my family sometimes, but homesick, no, I don't think so. Why? Are you feeling homesick?"

She shook her head. "No, I just wondered about you, all of you. It must be a long time since you left your homes and families."

"If you knew the sort of homes and families some of these kids left behind, you wouldn't ask the question."

"You didn't have such an awful family."

"No, but I was never particularly happy at home."

"Are you happy now?"

"I guess so. I'm not unhappy anyway."

"You're lucky. You grew up in a society that lets its children be independent from an early age. Our society believes in keeping children tied to their parents' apron strings."

They were about to leave the main bazaar street and take the turning that would take them to Mountainview when Tony noticed the group under the trees that bordered the street at the far end. He saw somebody and waved.

"Hi, Mark." His voice had a lilt in it that she had not heard before. "When did you get here, boy?"

They embraced and Mark said laughing, "Just now on the bus." He was a tall blond with a wide thin mouth and small blue eyes. Not good-looking like Tony but with a vitality which was magnetic.

She felt annoyed that Tony had without even a word of apology interrupted their conversation, and she was angry with Mark for being the cause of it. Now I am being jealous, she told herself. What next? What is Tony to me? Nothing. I don't even know him. I'm not even sure I like him very much.

She sat watching, listening, wishing she could be part of them and not an outsider looking in. They were in high spirits, animatedly talking, laughing, basking in Mark's presence. She had never seen them like this. At times she had wondered whether they enjoyed life at all. Apparently they needed somebody to provide a stimulus.

Abruptly, the talk and laughter came to a stop. Half a dozen policemen seemed to materialize from nowhere and came down the street clearing it of hippies. They were being quite rough, not intentionally cruel, but simply treating the hippies as though they were of no account. They were shouting at them, pushing them, sometimes bodily lifting and taking them away when they did not move fast enough. Sagar's group was walking into the woods when the policemen reached them, but they still pushed at some of the stragglers and sent them stumbling headlong. Sagar herself had not been touched, but she felt quite shaken by the experience. Apparently the Chief Minister was coming and the police had been ordered to clear the main road of the riff-raff.

The hippies did not seem affected. They went on chatting as though nothing very extraordinary had happened. Sagar thought, it's the price they pay for anonymity. They have spurned a privileged position in society and opted for this life of flotsam, being kicked this way and that by their own whim, circumstances and policemen. They are like ascetics practising self-mortification in order to go beyond pain and pleasure, to attain Nirvana. But they had not yet reached the state of supreme indifference. They were unsure and self-involved. Anyway, she didn't think they aimed at supreme indifference.

## 13

That evening they had music. Mark had brought his guitar, and he strummed it while they all sang. They built a fire outdoors and sat around it. Sagar was delighted to find that she knew some of their songs. She joined in softly. She smelled the fragrant fire, watching the flames leap up and pick out a pair of dreamy eyes or a shining cheek or a glint of white teeth. She sat close to Tony and they had their arms around each other. She felt warm and happy, in consonance with everything around her. She thought, why can't I always feel like this? But finally the music stopped and they let the fire die down and she got up reluctantly. She was cold and stiff, and even after they went inside, she continued shivering under her blankets.

"Tony."

"Yeah."

"I can't get warm."

"Come in with me, then."

She moved close to him, feeling a little self-conscious. The warmth of his body soon warmed her, but she felt reluctant to move away. She had not been this close to a man, ever. She had sometimes wanted to with Nitin, but he had always held himself aloof, and she had not wanted to take the initiative, for fear of being spurned, or worse, mocked.

There was restless movement around them. Someone lit a cigarette and passed it round. She smelled the now familiar smell and said, "What's it like, to smoke marijuana?"

"Makes you feel good."

"Good how?"

"Relaxed, happy."

"Why do you need marijuana to feel relaxed and happy?" She wanted to add that she felt relaxed and happy without it, right now.

"Who needs it?"

"Then why do you smoke it?"

"Why do you eat?"

"To fill my belly of course. I couldn't survive without eating."

"You could survive by eating dry bread and nothing else. Why do you eat all the other things? Because they taste good, right?"

There was a difference but she couldn't put it into words. She felt a little impatient with herself. Why couldn't she leave things be? Why did she feel this need to question, compare, judge?

She said, "Does it have any bad effect on you? Like making you sick or dizzy?"

He laughed softly. "It doesn't on me, but it probably will on you, 'cause you're so scared."

"Don't laugh at me, Tony."

She felt near tears. The earlier mood had vanished and she felt the grating of struggle, dissonance.

"I'm not laughing at you, kid," he said. In the dark he turned her face to him and kissed her gently on the mouth. She was deeply stirred by the kiss, but she was afraid of her own feelings.

Someone struck a match and guiltily she turned her face away from Tony. What she saw in the flare of the match froze her. She had read about it in clinical detail in a book her mother had given her, and later in other books the purpose of which was not dispensing knowledge to adolescents; she had heard about it in carefully veiled references, evasive answers to her questions, snickering jokes; she had thought about it. Yet she had never quite believed that this was what it was like, two bodies obscenely locked together in the presence of dozens of people, rocking, straining, and a face with almost a snarl upon it.

Then as darkness thankfully enveloped her again, she felt her face flaming with horror and shame. She moved quietly back under her own covers. Tony said nothing at all and she wondered if she had disappointed him.

She thought, with tears of anger and self-disgust starting in her eyes, what am I doing here? All this was only a worthless gesture, nothing more. If I hold a mirror up to myself, it will show me my mother's face. That is why they went away. They were sure of themselves, sure of me. They merely gave me the chance to find out what they knew all along. I am their daughter.

## 14

Gautam had tortured himself for days, imagining Sagar alone and frightened in strange places, or dying of some horrible accident or disease, or staring at him without recognition, her mind ruined by drugs. There were times when he thought it would be better to have a child die rather than something like this happen. Then he felt ashamed of himself, thinking that it was the height of selfishness to wish Sagar dead because his imagination tortured him.

He wrote a poem about her, feeling that the writing of it expressed his impotence, his inadequacy. He put it at the back of a drawer where Rohini would not chance upon it. It was the first time he had withheld from her a piece of his own writing. It was symptomatic of the relationship they had built by skirting the inaccessible areas.

Rohini seemed determined that they should not talk about Sagar. In a way he resented this, but he knew that there was good sense in it. Nothing could be accomplished by talking about Sagar. Rohini was now in control of herself, easily and confidently taking up the threads of their life. Perhaps it was the familiar environment that gave her strength. He felt somehow a faint regret that she had made such a good job of putting the pieces together. It was as if there had been a mould of the old Rohini waiting at the flat and once she returned, she could fit herself back into it easily.

They worked on the magazine, read, went to plays, browsed in bookshops, gave and attended parties. The normalcy of their life had a lulling effect. There were periods when Gautam did not think about Sagar at all. When he did, his thoughts were almost benign. After all, nothing so terrible had happened. It was just hysteria that had given rise to all the morbid fancies. He began to get quite used to not having Sagar around. He even accepted her absence as more or less permanent. He realized this when Sagar finally came back.

They were having a small dinner party. The door chimes rang and Gautam thought, who can that be, I think everyone's here. He opened the door without any premonition, and when he saw Sagar, he realized with a shock that he had really begun to think in terms of her never returning.

She looked dirty and inexpressibly tired. Also she seemed to have lost some weight. He wanted to take in his arms and hold her tight and tell her that he was happy she had come back. But he stood staring at her and the moment passed.

He only said, "Sagar, come in."

She walked in without a word, carrying her small suitcase.

He said, "Are you all right?" and she said, in a slightly impatient voice, "Of course I'm all right."

She had to pass through the living room to get to her bedroom. The conversation stopped when everyone saw her. She didn't look at anyone or greet anyone. She saw out of the corner of her eye that her mother had got up but she didn't stop to say hello.

A woman's voice said, "Where is she coming from? Didn't she come back with you?"

59

There was something more than simple curiosity in the voice. Rohini said smoothly, "No, she decided to stay on."

"I see."

Rohini went on, in the same casual voice, "Actually, she wanted to stay with some hippies, you know."

"No. Really?"

"Yes, why not? She was intrigued by them, and she wanted to see what they were like, so we decided to let her. One should expose oneself to all sorts of experiences, don't you think?"

The woman said with something like awe in her voice, "I'd love to hear what it was like."

Rohini said, "Maybe she will join us later, if she's not too tired."

Sagar turned to the large bedroom window which looked out on the ocean. The Ocean looked alive in the moonlight, like an enormous menacing animal. She could see the sinuous movement of the waves as they built up for a powerful crash, but she knew the crash would never come because the rollers broke on a sand bar several yards from the beach. She watched them break and come tamely to slap against the beach, ending in gentle laughter, and the tension in her grew into a big red ball and then broke into millions of fragments as she hurled the suitcase she still carried through the open window. Then she went like a fury through the room, picking up anything she could, jars of cream, comb, brush from her dressing table, clothes from the chest of drawers, covers and pillows from the bed, shoes, books, a chair, and throwing them all down to crash on the beach six storeys below.

# PEANUTS FOR THE MONKEYS

While she and Brijesh stood by the suitcases which the customs inspector was opening for a cursory look, she caught a glimpse of her mother-in-law beyond the barrier, and the child in her arms. The child seemed to have no relationship to the child of her imagination, or even to the child of the photographs on whom, after all, her imagination was superimposed. She thought, if it were someone else's child, I wouldn't give him a second glance, and then looked around guiltily, as if her fleeting thought had in some way been mirrored on her face for all to read.

She had counted the days to get back to him. During the last few months she had crossed off the days on her calendar. She had trained herself to let days go by without looking at the calendar, and then, with a delicious feeling of having sneaked up on herself, crossing off a whole lot of dates at once. The feeling of time moving in sudden jumps was easier to live with than the feeling of it moving at a regular, plodding pace.

As she walked towards the barrier she was thinking, what should I do? Should I just smile at him, or say his name, or ask him some question? Should I take him from her? What is a four-year-old doing being carried anyway? Will he come to me? She told herself, don't be silly. Just act natural. She put down her shoulder bag and the suitcase she was carrying, tucked her giant purse under her arm, and held her arms out for him. He looked at her, it seemed, without recognition, and shrank away, hiding his face into his grandmother's neck. Preeti felt the hot flush of humiliation spread over her face and neck and told herself, after all, you have been away for two years, how can you expect him to recognize you when those two years represent half his life? But as she bent down to pick up the bags she was thinking, but isn't there some sort of instinctive recognition, some trace of a learned response on his brain?

During the day she tended to observe him objectively. A skinny child, pale, coy, self-conscious. Dressed in ill-fitting clothes — loose, too-long shorts and a really ghastly yellow bush-shirt with brass buttons all over the front. Good God! You would think she might have dressed him in one of the lovely outfits I sent for him. He talked in a whining, demanding voice, he threw food about while his grandmother tried to coax a few mouthfuls into him.

That night, lying on the bed with its not very clean linen, its hard pillow which was giving her a crick in the neck, she said miserably to Brijesh, "He won't even call me Aai. Shouldn't your mother at least have taught him that? He calls her Aai."

"Many children call their grandmother that. You can have him call you Mummy. What difference does it make what he calls you?"

"And he is so thin."

Brijesh said, smiling, "After two years of seeing fat American children, he's bound to look thin to you."

"It's not just his thinness. He doesn't look quite healthy."

"Oh Vikram's all right. Lots of children are underweight. It has nothing to do with their health."

"And the hours he is allowed to keep. What is a four-year-old doing eating dinner with us and not going to bed until after ten?"

Brijesh sighed. "Preeti, be reasonable. Lots of Indian children keep these kind of hours and nobody thinks it's so terrible. After all, the important thing was to have someone who would love him and care for him while you were away. Naturally, your ideas of child-rearing are different from Aai's. But she has done her best and I am sure no permanent harm has been done. Now he is all yours, and you can bring him up exactly as you like."

He did not say it, but it was there, implied always. If you had really cared how he was brought up, you wouldn't have left him. Even Brijesh could not get away from thinking that.

And Vikram is not all mine, she thought. Far from it. When they went to bed she had called him to her and he had refused to sleep on her bed, running to his grandmother and crying and carrying on as though he was being abducted. She could see her mother-in-law's triumphant expression while she cooed at the child to calm him, then patted him to sleep while he lay with his head in her lap.

Preeti lay on the sagging cot stiffly, long after Brijesh, snubbed in his efforts to awaken her to love, had gone to sleep. She listened to the sounds of traffic, of people, smelling the fumes of automobile exhaust, feeling the damp heat that was so familiarly Bombay, and finally fell asleep thinking of her son.

The next morning she awoke quite early, hearing Vikram's whining in his peculiar spoilt-child voice, amazed that he was up already. How can the child possibly get enough sleep, she thought. No wonder he looks so thin and nervous.

She went to the bathroom to wash her face and wrinkled her nose with distaste. It bore evidence, as did the rest of the flat, to the typical "It's only a rented place, why should we spend on maintaining it" mentality. The tiles were yellowed and cracked and the grime collected in the cracks could never be properly cleaned. And the place stank because it served the dual purpose of bathing place and urinal. Some day, she thought, we are going to get out of this place. Even though it was a near impossibility at least for years to come, she derived some solace from thinking it.

When she went to the kitchen she saw Vikram sitting at the table with a sullen look on his face and a cup of milk in front of him. She gave a bright smile and said, "Aren't you going to drink your milk?"

"No, I don't want it."

His grandmother said, "I'll put a little coffee in it, then will you drink it?"

Before he could answer, Preeti said, "You can't give coffee to such a small child. He'll drink it plain, won't you darling?"

"I won't." Vikram said.

"He is a very difficult child to feed," her mother-in-law said fondly. "I have the hardest time getting him to eat anything."

Preeti said, "Vikram, you had better drink that milk, and quickly."

He responded to the threat implied in her words, threw her a baleful look and drank the milk.

"Fine. You are a good boy. Now run along and play."

Vikram continued to sit stolidly at the table, making her feel like a fool. Her mother-in-law said, "Would you like some tea?"

"No, I'll have some later with Brijesh. Vikram, I'm going to unpack my big suitcase, do you want to come and help me? It's got all sorts of presents for you in it."

Vikram didn't budge but his face softened. The lure of a lot of presents was too much to withstand. He looked at his grandmother and she said, "Go along, Vickoo, see what your mother has brought you."

Well thank you, Preeti thought, for so graciously giving him permission to come with me. Vikram seemed delighted with the toys which she had painstakingly chosen for him, and when the unpacking was done, he gravely carried all of them to show his grandmother.

This became the pattern. Preeti could not assume control of Vikram without his co-operation and his grandmother was always there to see to it that he did not give it. Oh she was very smart, and very devious. On the surface she was sweet and persuasive, but she manoeuvred every situation to her own advantage and, Preeti thought, as she held the ace of spades in her hand, this was fairly easy.

Preeti said to Brijesh, "He will not come back to me as long as she is here."

"What do you suggest? That I throw her out?" Brijesh said with, Preeti thought, unwarranted nastiness. The also conformed to a pattern, established long before they left. Preeti knew that her mother-in-law disapproved of a number of things about her, but she never openly criticized. She expressed her disapproval in double-edged talk which Brijesh accepted as perfectly straightforward.

She had said, for instance, "Naturally, Preeti is in two minds about going because of the baby. But I think she should go. After all, since she does take her career seriously, this is too good a chance to miss. And I am here to take care of little Vickoo."

Brijesh had thought that his mother was extremely helpful and understanding. Only Preeti saw the barb in this little speech, because she had not been in two minds at all. The moment she had received Dr Walker's offer, she knew she would accept it. She had not even thought about Vikram until later. Brijesh had already planned his trip, and there was no question of his cancelling it. And she had to admit that it was her mother-in-law's offer to take care of Vikram that had made her trip possible. She was grateful for this, but felt that her mother-in-law had not been quite fair. Brijesh had been away for as long as she had, so theoretically, they should both be strangers to the child. Or if one of them was less of a stranger, it should be Preeti, since she had more to do with him than Brijesh before they left. But Preeti observed that Vikram was less wary, more friendly with his father, no doubt as a result of the grandmother's coaching.

One day Brijesh said, "I have a wonderful idea. Let's take Vickoo to the zoo."

"I wish you wouldn't use that horrible nickname," Preeti said fiercely. "If you could only hear how stupid and effeminate it sounds."

"All right, all right, don't get so worked up about it. If you don't like it I won't use it."

At first Vikram insisted that Aai and Nana go to the zoo with them.

Aai said, "I have no time to go with you today, Vickoo. And Nana has to go to work. Why don't you go with your father and mother? They will show you the lions and the monkeys. Father will buy you peanuts for the monkeys. And he will give you ice-cream, won't you, Brijesh?"

At the zoo when Brijesh bought a bag of peanuts from a vendor at the gate, Preeti said, "You mustn't feed the monkey really, you know, Vikram."

"Why?"

"Because this sign says that you mustn't feed any of the animals."

"But why?"

"Because if everyone feeds the animals they will get sick, the way you will get sick if you eat too much."

Vikram started crying. "Aai lets me feed the monkeys. I always feed the monkeys peanuts."

Brijesh said, "Let him just this once."

Taking this for permission, Vikram ran to the monkey cages. They followed more slowly.

"That was a good object lesson on how to undermine my authority."

"Look, above all you want to make friends with him, don't you? Discipline can wait till later."

"It's a sorry state of affairs when I have to bribe my son into liking me."

"You yourself said that you are something of a stranger to him —"

"But why? Wouldn't you think your mother would at least have shown him photographs and got him used to thinking of me as his mother?"

"She probably did, but it's difficult for a child to feel close to someone who is far away."

"You aren't willing to hear any criticism of your mother. You don't see that she is making it impossible for me to claim him as my son. I just knew something like this would happen."

Her voice had risen and he raised his above hers. "Then why the hell did you go and leave him?"

"It always comes back to that, doesn't it?" she said bitterly.

"I am sorry."

"What should I have done? Do you really think I should have thrown away the chance of a lifetime? Was it a crime to have put my work before my child? Didn't you do the same?"

"I said I am sorry, Preeti. Look, I think you are upsetting yourself unnecessarily. Aai wouldn't turn Vikram against you. You are too tense about it, and that probably scares him off. Just have patience, that's all."

From a distance they saw that Vikram had climbed inside the guard rail and was putting his arm inside a monkey cage. The monkey came to take the peanut pod from Vikram's hand and he suddenly withdrew it, teasing the animal.

"Vikram, don't do that," Preeti shouted, but he had already put his hand in the cage again, and before Brijesh could reach him the monkey had slapped it. This time Vikram had not been quick enough to withdraw his hand. He shrieked in pain. Luckily the monkey, not really interested in attacking, had withdrawn to the other side of the cage and Brijesh quickly picked up Vikram and walked away from the gathering crowd. They found that Vikram was not badly hurt. There were a couple of deep scratches on his forearm which they washed and dressed with the help of the first aid box in the superintendent's office. But Vikram had been badly frightened and would not stop crying, even after the offer of ice-cream. He kept saying, "I want to go home to Aai." Finally they took him home.

Grandmother said, "What happened? A monkey? Vickoo, you are a naughty boy. How many times have I told you not to put your hand in the cage? All right, all right, don't cry. Come to Aai, she will take away your hurt."

Preeti went to her room and in a little while she heard Vikram's sobs stop. Brijesh came in. "Phew, that was a close call. That monkey could have mauled him."

"If it had, your mother would have been responsible for it."

"You don't know what you are saying."

"I know very well. She plans these things."

"My God, you really are unbalanced. How could she be responsible for anything when she wasn't even there?"

"She took care not to warn us about his putting his hand in the monkey cage."

"We should have been watching him more closely. Let's face it. It was our carelessness."

"Here too. You heard her. She knows he always tries to do that. She should have warned us to watch him, but she chose not to. And if you are going to tell me that it wasn't intentional —"

Brijesh said in a voice trembling with anger, "Have you any suggestion as to why she might be doing this?"

"She wants to steal him from me."

"What on earth for? What would she want with such a small child?"

"So she can get back at me by making him hate me. She has never liked me, never liked the fact that you married me without consulting her."

"Preeti, I don't want to hear any more. You are saying things you will be sorry for when you come to your senses. Where are you going?"

"Out. I can't stand being under the same roof with all of you."

She came back late and said she had a headache and didn't want any dinner. She slept, and woke sometime during the night to see Brijesh already in bed, fast asleep. She lay there for a while, feeling her stomach sending messages that it needed food. Restlessly she got out of bed and wandered around the flat. She looked into the other bedroom and saw her mother-in-law sleeping with her arm around the little bundle that was Vikram. She whirled away and went back to her bedroom. Brijesh was gently snoring and his undisturbed sleep added to her fury. She took off her clothes and flung them down in a heap. Then she whipped the cover off him and got into bed with him.

He said drowsily, "What? Preeti?"

Then he felt her nakedness with his hands and came instantly awake.

"Preeti, oh darling. I love you so."

He pulled her close hungrily and she thought, "I hate this and I hate you, but you are going to give me a baby. It will be my first child, and it will be mine utterly."

# ASK NO QUESTIONS

The victim died without regaining consciousness. That's what the papers would say when they reported the accident.

Kamal looked at the dead body of her sister and then at the man beside her. He looked gray, and she felt sorry for him. And for Sangeeta. She had hoped that Sangeeta would say something before death claimed her, but from the moment the car hit her, Sangeeta had been concerned only with the business of her own dying.

When Kamal had brought Sangeeta home after their mother's death, she had been very apologetic about it. Having Sangeeta live with them was going to put a strain on their modest income and their small flat. Then she found that only she was voicing all the objections and Anant and the children accepted Sangeeta's presence immediately and without reservations. She then thought resentfully, it's all right for Anant to be generous about it. He has an earning wife after all. Anant worked as a laboratory assistant in a sugar factory and she supplemented his salary by running a nursery school for the children in the factory colony. She managed the family finances with skill and efficiency and believed in the future for which she saved every paisa she felt they could spare.

For weeks Sangeeta was inconsolable. She never talked about her mother or in any way shared her grief. She simply stared into space, not bothering to dry the tears which flowed down her cheeks.

"Sangeeta behaves as though it's her own private loss," Kamal said. "She was my mother too."

"Her death can't mean the same to you, Kamal. After all, you have me and the children. She has no one else."

The Sangeeta who finally emerged from her lonely mourning baffled Kamal even more. Her mood changed unpredictably, from gay and full of chatter one moment to tears and a sulky silence the next. With patience and understanding, Kamal weathered this. The next phase, however, tried her patience to breaking point. Sangeeta would tell her, in a coy and slightly self-deprecatory voice, about men who had been attracted to her. There was a balding middle-aged history professor who had been madly in love with her.

"How do you know he was in love with you?" Kamal asked sceptically.

"Did he tell you so"

"Of course not. He didn't have to. It was obvious, the way he looked at me in class. Everyone remarked on it."

"Was that all?"

Sangeeta refused to be dampened by her sister's lack of enthusiasm. She swung her braid forward over her shoulder and curling the end over her finger said, "He was fat and short and had a wife and three kids." She giggled.

One day she said, "Did I ever tell you about this photographer? He said I had a terrific figure. I should do fashion modelling."

Slender and graceful, she pirouetted for her sister's benefit.

"Do you suppose I could go back to Bombay and work as a model? I'd love to."

"We'll see about that after you finish college."

Anant just laughed it off. That was his way of dealing with problems. Pretend they didn't exist at all.

"Why does she tell such preposterous lies?" Kamal said. "I find it very disturbing."

"All children indulge in a bit of fantasy."

"She is not a child, Anant. She is only eight years younger than I."

"Is that all? She seems young for her age."

71

One day Kamal found Sangeeta in a flood of tears and it took her a long time and nearly all her patience to coax the reason out of her.

"I know I am a burden to you," Sangeeta said sobbing, "but I've nowhere else to go."

"Nonsense. Have I ever made you feel that you are a burden?"

"No, but you are my sister. There's no reason why Anantrao should have to put up with me."

"What do you mean, child? Has he said something to you?"

"Oh he didn't say anything. I just feel that he doesn't want me here."

"Something must have happened to make you feel that."

"Nothing's happened."

"Then you are just letting your imagination run wild. Of course Anant wants you here. He likes you."

"How can you say he likes me when he never even notices me or talks to me?"

"Oh Sangeeta, he is just busy. And he is not a talkative man. Have you seen him talking to me very much? I'm the one who talks. He just listens."

Sangeeta persisted. "No, that's not it. He doesn't like my being here. After all, in this small place I must be in the way. And it must cost a lot to support me. I know Mother didn't leave much money."

'Now that's enough, Sangeeta. If you don't know any better than to talk such rot about someone who's been so generous to you, you had better just shut up."

Kamal thought Anant would laugh at this, but he didn't. He said gravely, "Poor child. She is right. I've been very thoughtless. We mustn't let her feel unwanted. After all, it can't be very nice for her to feel so utterly dependent on us."

Kamal noticed after this that Anant went out of his way to pay more attention to Sangeeta. He complimented her on a pretty sari, talked to her about her studies, laughed at her stories about her fellow-students. Sangeeta began to look much happier and Kamal was very grateful to Anant. There were not many husbands who would put up with a silly sister-in-law with such good grace.

One hot October afternoon after the nursery children had left, Kamal suddenly found that there were some things she had to buy before she cooked dinner. She left reluctantly. She was not usually so unorganized. When she came back hot and tired and irritated with herself, she found Sangeeta crying, she was in no mood to deal with her tears. She went straight to the kitchen and started cooking with as much noise as possible, to indicate to Sangeeta that there were more important things in the world than shedding tears over an imagined hurt.

Sangeeta came and stood near the stove, without offering to help. Kamal had decided not ask her what the matter was, but the silent tears wore down her determination.

"For heaven's sake, Sangeeta," she exploded, "if you want to tell me what's causing all the tears, be quick about it. Otherwise do your crying elsewhere. I can't stand your acting like a tragic heroine."

"I don't know how to tell you. It's about Anantrao. He doesn't behave properly with me."

"Will you please make yourself clear?"

"How can I make myself clearer? Can't you understand?"

"No, I'm afraid I can't," Kamal said coldly.

"All right. If you insist I'll spell it out for you. He tries to touch me, put his arms around me, kiss me, when we are alone in the house. He even came to me one night after everyone was asleep, but I sent him away."

"You are an incurable liar."

"No."

"First you weep because you feel that Anant doesn't like you. Then you turn around and accuse him of trying to seduce you! You should at least be consistent in your lying."

"I am not lying. I may have lied about other things, but not this. I swear I'm telling you the truth."

73

"I am waiting for your apology."

There was a long silence. Finally Sangeeta said, "All right. I'm sorry."

"And what you just told me is a lie?"

"It's a lie?"

During dinner Sangeeta was sullen and silent. Her eyes were red and swollen and she kept them riveted to her plate while she pecked at her food.

"Is anything wrong, Sangeeta?" Anant asked her.

"No."

"Aren't you feeling well?"

"I'm all right, there's nothing wrong with me," Sangeeta said stiffly.

He looked at Kamal inquiringly but she just pursed her lips and shook her head. I'd like to hear what he says when I tell him about her latest fantasy, she thought.

Later she found that she was postponing leaving the kitchen long after she had finished clearing up. I can't talk casually about it, she thought. I'll tell him in a few days when I am calmer about it.

In the morning when she did her hair she pushed her face up close to the mirror. There's still no gray in my hair, she thought. But there are lines at the corners of my mouth and eyes. And my eyes look tired and dull. Not sparkling like her eyes. Does she put something on them to make them sparkle so? And my face is gaunt, the bones seem to stand out more because I pull my hair back tight. Sangeeta's cheeks are soft and rounded and she lets her hair frame her face so prettily. Suppose I did my hair the way she does, in a loose plait down my back instead of in a tight bun? No, that's foolish. Why should I have to use silly feminine wiles to win Anant back from her?

While having morning tea Kamal looked at Sangeeta and suddenly felt old and haggard and used. Was the girl looking prettier these days? Well, looking pretty is not all I have to think about, she told herself. I am a person, not a pretty thing to be enjoyed by a man. I have stood at Anant's side as his equal and made this life possible by working as hard as he does. If I am tired and old before my time, it's from doing his housework and bearing his children. And now if he falls for a pretty face . . .

Stop it, she admonished herself. I must be mad to think these things. Sangeeta was lying of course. I never believed her for a minute. I must tell Anant about it tonight and have a good laugh with him.

But suppose he doesn't laugh? What then?

Stop it.

She watched Anant. But more closely she watched Sangeeta. Perhaps it's true, she thought, that deep in your heart you always hate brothers and sisters. They are always your rivals in everything. It seems as though I have always hated Sangeeta. She was always the pretty one, the smart one, the one Mother showed off to friends. She even had a pretty name. Kamal thought back to her childhood and remembered the bitter taste of hate.

Sometimes she would look at Sangeeta and think, "I mustn't let her do this to me. She is bad, but I don't hate her. I pity her. She invents these stories because she has nothing else in life."

On night Sangeeta was coughing and Anant said, "That's a bad cough. Do we have any cough drops?"

"There might be a few left in the packet I bought for Prakash."

Anant found the cough drops and went to give them to Sangeeta. Kamal tiptoed after him. Standing by the door of the children's room she saw Anant bend over the girl, hand her the cough drops, speak softly to her so as not to wake the children. Kamal turned and went back to bed then, and Anant came back a few seconds later. Had he touched her, kissed her, in those few seconds? Had he told her he loved her?

"Kamal," he called softly but she pretended to be asleep. I can't face him or his love with these thoughts in my mind, she thought. It is funny, my feeling guilty because of what I am thinking. It is he who should feel guilty. Men are horrible. They can cheat their wives and then face them cheerfully as though nothing out of the ordinary had happened.

Anant called again and she thought in sudden panic, why is he so persistent? Does he want to tell me he is in love with my sister and wants a divorce? No, I won't let him say it. I will not be condemned to a lonely life for no fault of mine. She did not reply and finally he went to his own bed.

I wish she would die, Kamal thought. Over and over she repeated the thought until its presence ceased to shock her.

Now Sangeeta was dead. She was a body which would soon be released by the hospital. And Anant had just come in. They had finally been able to reach him and he had come running. As soon as he came in, Kamal found herself suddenly alert, every nerve in her body tense to see, to feel. Anant stood with his back to her, looking down at Sangeeta. Except for a few scratches and bruises, the face was quite unmarred.

It was a long time before she said, "Anant."

He put a hand out and touched Sangeeta's cheek gently. When he turned his face looked gray and haggard, and there were white patches around his mouth and nose.

He could have lost a sister or a daughter, Kamal thought. Or a well-loved friend. Or a sweetheart.

"Will you miss her?" she asked.

"Of course I'll miss her. She had become such a part of the family."

"She was so pretty."

"Yes."

"Did you like her, Anant? Did you like her a lot?"

"Of course I liked her."

Words, she thought. They are only sounds. They only mean something when you want them to mean something.

She started crying then. She felt him take a step towards her. When he didn't come any closer she looked up.

"Sangeeta is dead," she said.

"Yes."

She met his eyes then and saw the pity in them and hid her face from him. She knew that his pity was not for Sangeeta.

# DISTORTED HEAVEN

Neelam was bathing the baby, her sari tucked up and wet, her hair still undone, her face streaked with perspiration from the warm steamy air of the bathroom, when the doorbell rang. Vasant opened the door.

"Neelam," he called, "where are you?"

"I'm giving Sanju her bath. What is it?"

"Have you almost finished?"

His voice did not sound anxious, but there was something in it which told her to expect news of some consequence.

"Dry her and put her clothes on," she said, handing the baby to the maid.

Vasant had a telegram in his hand which he wordlessly handed to her. She held a corner of the oblong pink paper in her damp fingers and read the message. She let her hand drop to her side and looked at Vasant. He stood rigid and expectant, waiting for some comment from her. But she didn't say anything.

"What are you thinking about?" he finally asked her.

"About the strange kind of justice in the nature of events, if only one is prepared to wait long enough for it."

"Don't call it justice," his voice was harsh. "Maybe you have finally got your revenge by letting her die a lonely broken woman. Was it worth it?"

She considered the question.

"No. No, I can't say it was. Revenge never is, is it? The moment I read the telegram I wished I had gone and made my peace with her. But she didn't ask for me. She was too proud. And now, of course, it's too late."

"I've often wondered," Vasant said musingly, "what she was like as a young girl. Sometimes I feel I can almost see her and then she eludes me."

A young law student sat in his rented room, reading a letter aloud to a girl.

"They are a good and well-known family, and the girl is suitable in every way," he read. "It would be a good connection. I hope you will contact them and see the girl and let us know your decision. We have seen the girl and approve of her. But the final decision rests with you."

He concluded with a laugh. The girl did not laugh. She looked down at her feet and said nothing.

"Aruna?"

"Um."

"You are not taking this seriously, are you?"

"Your parents are. This is the third letter in two months."

"I turned down the other two offers. I'll turn down this one too."

"How long can you keep dodging the issue, Manohar? They are determined to get you married this season and they will keep on trying as long as you allow them to."

He felt a hot blush rise to his face. He had been hoping to postpone this moment. He knew his parents would never approve of Aruna, and he couldn't afford to antagonize them before he was able to earn a decent living.

"You are right, Aruna," he said. "I'm going to tell them about us. I'll write immediately." He was thinking that he would not immediately have to tell them that Aruna was the daughter of a rehabilitated Devdasi. There could still be a few days' respite, and he would have more time to think about a plan. "Why are you looking so sad?"

"Maybe I am taking too much for granted."

"Now you are the coward."

"No. I just don't want you to regret anything."

"I won't, so long as you don't."

The girl lifted her delicate oval face and smiled at him.

After she left Manohar began to pace the room. He knew he ought to go and eat, but he didn't feel like it. He had thought

79

that coming to a decision would give him relief from the tension of the past few months, but he felt no relief. His own restlessness disturbed him, because he felt that by being less than completely confident about the future he was being disloyal to Aruna.

When he heard the knocking he said absentmindedly, "Come in."

The door opened and on the threshold stood the most beautiful girl he had ever seen. She was exquisitely slender and tall, and she moved into the room with the grace of a dancer.

"You are Manohar Rege?" Her voice was quiet and slightly husky, not the kind of voice he would have expected her to have. It should have been gentle and musical.

"Yes. I don't seem to recognize you. Should I?"

"No, I don't think you have ever seen me. But you would have soon, if you intended to follow your parents' instructions."

"So you are Sumitra."

"Yes."

"Well?"

"I had reason to believe that you did not intend to follow your parents' instructions. I know about you and Aruna, you see."

"I was not trying to keep it a secret."

"Please don't be offended. I didn't mean it that way. I have come to ask you a favour."

There was no flippancy in her talk. She talked with a serious, intent face, watching him all the time.

"Why don't you stop talking in riddles and come to the point?"

"I want you to marry me."

"What? Do you know what you are saying?"

She smiled faintly, as though she had expected the outburst.

"I know."

"What you are asking is impossible. You said you knew about me and Aruna. Then you ought to know that I am going to marry her."

Suddenly Sumitra started crying. She cried with complete abandon, and her tears were oddly at variance with her earlier poise. He felt sorry for her.

"Don't cry," he said. "Tell me what the matter is. I'll help you."

"There is only one way in which you can help me."

"I see."

"I think you have guessed it, haven't you?"

"Who was it?"

"Someone who's worked for my father for a number of years. A clerk. But that's beside the point."

"Did he —"

"No. Putting all the blame on him isn't going to help me. And in any case I can't plead complete innocence."

"Do your parents know anything of this?"

"Oh no. My father will kill me if he found out."

"Isn't there anything you can do?"

"I know there are ways of dealing with my condition, but I don't know how to go about it, whom to contact. And I don't see how I can possibly manage it without anyone finding out."

"Why can't you marry him?"

"He is already married, has three children. Anyway, it's out of the question. I couldn't marry him."

Under the circumstances her arrogance seemed ridiculous. It would have been offensive if it hadn't been so casually expressed.

"So you're asking me to marry you. Tell me, what makes you think I might even consider it?"

"I'm not asking you to give up Aruna. If you marry me and give my child a name, I'll leave you absolutely free to go on seeing her."

"What makes you think she will agree to such an arrangement?"

"If you agree, she has no choice. Being what she is, such an arrangement shouldn't seem strange to her. I know you are going to say I am no better than she is, perhaps worse. But that's not the point. I would be much more of an asset to you as a wife than she can be."

"How did you find out about us?"

"I have a cousin who is in your college. When he heard about the negotiations going on between our families, he told me this. You may think you are carrying on your affair in secret, but everyone knows about it. Of course my cousin told me about it from quite different motives. He expected me to turn you down."

"But you thought you could use this information in some way to make me marry you instead. You still haven't answered my question. Give me one reason why you think I should agree."

"Well, you can't deny that you are ambitious. Otherwise you would have defied your family and married her long ago."

"I couldn't have supported us."

"You could have left college and taken a job. When you want to do something badly enough, you can always find a way. But I can't see you giving up your whole life for her. You are not the type, and you were realistic enough to realize that. The fact that you haven't married her all these days is proof enough of what I am saying."

Suddenly he was angry. "I've heard enough. I don't know why I have put up with you as long as I have. I should have thrown you out long ago, but I am doing it now. Get out and stay out of my life. I never want to set eyes upon you again."

Unpredictably she smiled "Do you know why you are angry? Nobody likes to face the truth about himself, especially when the truth is unpleasant."

He looked at her with loathing. "Get out this instant. If you were not a woman, I would have thrown you out bodily."

"I'll go. But think about it. Here's my phone number. Get in touch with me when you realize that I am offering you the only solution to all our problems. Only don't be too long. I can't afford to wait."

When he called her a few days later he said, "You realize that if I agree to marry you, I'll hold you to your promise about Aruna?"

"Of course."

"There's only one more thing. The child must be brought up without the knowledge that I am not its real father."

Vasant said, "I do know of course that she was beautiful. Even at forty, when I first met her, she was a rarely beautiful woman. What I wonder about is what kind of a person she was inside, to have made such a preposterous bargain with a man she didn't even know, and stuck to it. She could have left your father later."

"I don't know why she didn't," Neelam said. "I never really knew her.

Sanju had been brought into the room and deposited on the rug. Neelam watched her playing. I, too, must once have played happily like you, she thought. But you are lucky, you and your brother. You are whole. Some children are born lame or blind or with a heart defect. But there are other things, less tangible things, that can be just as surely crippling.

"It was the summer we got engaged when everything went wrong," she said. "I wonder if our engagement had anything to do with it."

"Why should it?"

"I think she was jealous of my happiness, and that suddenly goaded her into doing what she did. I remember she had been quite ill, with bleeding, pain, female troubles. She had been very irritable and snappy. She started nagging me for spending so much time with you and coming home late. She said if we couldn't keep away from each other what was keeping us from getting married immediately. When I told her that we had decided to wait until you had finished college, she thought that that was a lame excuse and asked Father to make me either marry you or stop seeing you. She said people were talking and if we finally didn't marry, it would be hard for me to find another husband. I just laughed, and Father told her that I was old enough to decide these things for myself, and he was not going to interfere. She was furious. But this was one of the things I loved about him. He knew how to allow a child to grow up and not keep her smothered in parental protection."

"You always worshipped him."

"Yes. Mother sometimes said jokingly that she was jealous of me, because her husband loved me more than he loved her."

"It must have been a bitter disappointment to her that the love he gave you was never extended to include her. Very ironical in a way."


"I want to talk to you," Sumitra said. She had never used his name and he had never insisted that she should. He looked at her, surprised. During their twenty years together, she had rarely entered his study when he was there. They had never discussed anything except Neelam, who had been their sole meeting point. At first Sumitra had been glad to see that Manohar was so fond of her daughter. She had been afraid that he would hate the child that had forced him to marry the mother. But then she saw that Neelam was only to be used as another weapon against her.

"Come in and sit down," Manohar said. "What is it?"

"I am going to ask you to give up Aruna." She came straight to the point.

"What?" Whatever he had expected, it was not this.

"Don't you think twenty years is long enough for us to have kept this ridiculous bargain?"

"As far as I can remember," he said mildly, "our bargain didn't have a time limit."

"I am asking you to put one on it now."

"What right do you have to ask me anything?"

"I am your wife."

"Only in name."

"That's true, and you've never let me forget it." She gave a short laugh. "I thought you were kind. I came to you because I was afraid of society's condemnation. But you have condemned me to a fate worse than any I could have imagined. Don't you think two decades of punishment is enough for any crime?"

"Punishment? Have I punished you? I have given your child a name. I have given you security, a home, status — everything you could ask for."

"Everything, except the essentials. Do you think I could really be satisfied with what you have given?"

"That was all you had asked for."

"I was not in a position to ask for more. I was young, inexperienced, and desperate. I had no bargaining power. I had to accept the minimum. I never thought that you would hold me rigidly to my promise for so long. I thought, with time, you would learn to love me. I thought we could be happy together in spite of having started out wrong. We could have been, if you had given us a chance. But you refused to. You have been cruel and selfish."

He felt an impersonal kind of pity for her, nothing more. He said, "My dear, calling me names is not going to help you. And you are forgetting that there is a third person involved in this, aren't you? She could have had a life of her own. She gave up everything for my sake."

"She has had a good life, and you, for twenty years. Isn't that a sufficient reward for her great and noble sacrifice?"

"What do you want me to do?"

"Settle some money on her. I am not saying that you should leave her destitute. But don't see her any more. Ask her to go away from here. Give me a few years of your life."

He thought he had done well by her. He was shocked at her ingratitude.

"It's out of the question," he said.

"Is that your last word?"

"Yes."

"Then there's only one thing left for me to do. I am going to tell Neelam about her real father."

"You wouldn't dare."

"Wouldn't I? Wait and see. You hold all the cards. I've nothing to punish you with except Neelam."

Suddenly he felt himself breaking out in a sweat.

"Give me time to think about it."

"I have given you twenty years."

"You keep throwing the twenty years in my face as though you've done me a favour by giving them to me."

"I'll give you one week."

"You know this is blackmail."

"You leave me no choice."

What mystified him was why Sumitra had suddenly decided that she could no longer put up with something she had accepted with equanimity and — he had to admit it — grace, for so long.


"I have wondered about Aruna too," Neelam said. "Sometimes, after Father's death, I wanted to go and see her, because she was the person closest to him. She shared the other half of his life, the one I knew nothing about. I saw her only once, the day Father died, at the cremation grounds. I saw this strange woman standing a little distance away from everyone, weeping inconsolably, and wondered who she could be."

"Why haven't you ever tried to find her and talk to her?"
"I was afraid to."
"You were afraid of disillusionment."
"Perhaps. I was also afraid of the unknown. I didn't want to discover a man whom I couldn't recognize as my father. I wanted whatever was left of my world to stay intact."

When Manohar went to see Aruna that evening, he felt that history was repeating itself. He was not sure any longer who was at the receiving end of life.

Aruna opened the door and he stepped into the flat which he had rented and furnished for her and which had been more of a home to him than the other. She was her usual self, calm and smiling, though with a veil of sadness which had never lifted from her all these years, as though she knew the inevitable end. And so, that summer evening, she was not really surprised when she heard what he had to tell her.

"You must do whatever you think is right," she said.
"But it's not merely my decision."
"I think it is. It always has been. I can't take the responsibility for making up your mind."
"What will you do?" he asked her, watching her. Time had not been as kind to her as it had been to Sumitra. She had grown heavy and her dark complexion had lost all its youthful freshness. Even her face, once delicate, had now become fleshy. She looked matronly, whereas Sumitra still looked virginal.

So you have already decided, she thought.

She said, "I'll probably go to my mother. She is old and ailing and needs someone to look after her."

She looked at him with a faintly sardonic smile.
"You really won't mind?" he asked.
"I am not in a position to mind, am I?"
"If that's the way you feel, we'll forget about it."

87

"And have you hate me? There couldn't be anything between us unless it was based on love and trust. Once that is gone, there is no point in dragging on an empty relationship."

"Do you think he committed suicide?" Neelam asked.

"No, I don't think so," Vasant said. "There was some suspicion of it, but there is often talk of that sort when an accident seems inexplicable. All we know is that he was crossing the street to reach his parked car, and walked right in front of a bus."

"I've always thought it was intentional."

"And you have held your mother responsible for it, haven't you? You thought she drove him to suicide."

"Neelam, you've got to pull yourself together."

Neelam stared unseemingly at the ceiling. She lay in her bed most of the time, getting out of it only to attend to her body's minimum needs.

"Why don't you do your hair and put on a fresh sari? Then you and Vasant can go out somewhere."

"I don't want to go out."

"For Vasant's sake you have to make an effort, Neelam. You own it to him. It's unnatural to mourn your father for such a long time."

"Don't teach me anything about what I owe Vasant. I hope I will never be in your position, but if I am, I am sure that I will mourn my husband more than you seem to be mourning yours. It's not I who am unnatural, it's you. Have you no tears for him? I've never seen you cry. Don't people cry for something they have lost?"

"I lost something I never had. He gave me everything except the one thing I wanted — love. That he gave to another."

"You've no right to slander him now that he is dead."

"This is not slander. This is the truth and it's time you faced it."

"That's enough, Mother. I don't want to hear anything more."

Neelam was suddenly afraid. She looked at her mother, saw the well-cut, slightly severe face, the fair colouring, the green-brown eyes now becoming yellow with age.

"That's right," Sumitra said harshly. "Take a good look at me. You've never really seen me, have you? He was always everything to you. It's almost funny, when you consider that he was not even your father." She smiled softly to herself. "You're not even his child."

"You must be out of your mind," Neelam cried. But she knew there was no escape. She had to hear what her mother had to say. And she knew that what her mother was telling her was the truth.


Neelam said, "I couldn't understand why, after keeping it from me for so long, she felt she must reveal it then. Once Father was dead, there was nothing she could gain by telling me."

"Perhaps she wanted to shock you out of your depression. Perhaps she only wanted to strike out blindly because she had been hurt."

"So she struck out at me. And tried to destroy me. My own mother. Except for your unexpected arrival that day, I might not be alive today."

"Don't blame that on her. You alone were responsible for it. You weren't strong enough to face the truth about yourself, and you took it for granted that I was not strong enough."

"There was no question of strength. I didn't think I had any right to let you marry the offspring of a scrupulous affair between a bored rich girl and an unscrupulous servant. I didn't think I could expose you to the sordidness of it."

"And you didn't think it was necessary to let me decide for myself."

"I know now that I was wrong," she said in a low voice.

"You were wrong about a lot of things. Neelam, don't you see your mother was as much a victim as the weaver of the web? Her initial mistake was in making such a fantastic proposition, but your father was wrong too, and weak, in accepting the proposition. For him there were only two honourable things to do. Ask your mother to go to hell and marry Aruna. Or marry your mother and make a clean break with Aruna. But in order to keep his conscience clear on every count, he landed himself and both the women into an impossible situation. If he had acted out of real kindness rather than some ulterior motive of his own, he would have given his marriage a chance. Instead he pursued his mistaken romantic ideal. He wanted his marriage to remain a heroic sacrifice rather than become a happy marriage. And by shutting your mother out of your life he did you a wrong too. When he died, you lost both parents."

Neelam looked at him wonderingly.

"Why haven't you ever said these things to me?"

"I didn't feel, until now, that you were ready to hear them."

Neelam thought back to the moment when she regained consciousness in the hospital and refused to see her mother. Everyone said that she was still in shock, and she would recover later and ask for her mother. But she knew better. She knew it would be never again.

If he had said this to me, she thought, I would have gone to her. But would I have? It is only because she is dead that we have talked about it. And now there must be no more ifs, because now she has broken the chain of ifs.

# THE HUNTRESS

When she was introduced to him, Vicky thought, I wonder where Arati collects these crummy types. He was at least a hundred years old. And he wore a dhoti. How old-world can you get? And his patchy face was out of a ghost story.

"What sort of things do you write?" Vicky asked him.

"Mostly newspaper articles. But I have also written some short stories and two novels."

He had strange eyes. Big and sort of sleepy looking. Vicky felt him watching her and wished she had spent a bit more time in front of the mirror. But dressing up for one of Arati's dinner parties bored her.

"How do you happen to have a name Vicky?" he asked her. He had a very attractive voice, low and soft.

"It's really Malavika. Somehow it got shortened to Vicky."

"It suits you."

"I don't know. I didn't like Malavika then. Now I think it's so much more glamorous. But here I am stuck with Vicky."

"Don't worry. Someday there will be someone special and to him you will always be Malavika."

Vicky laughed. She was beginning to enjoy herself.

"You have a beautiful laugh. You should laugh oftener. Why do you look so sad?"

"You are imagining things."

"Am I? Is it disappointment in love?"

"Perhaps."

"The young man didn't keep his promises?"

He has a nerve, Vicky thought, But she said, "Frankly, there were no promises."

"What happened?"

"He went to England."

"And you haven't heard from him?"

91

She shook her head.

"Maybe he will write when he is settled there."

"He is settled enough to write, but not to me."

"Perhaps he is shy."

She laughed. "You have such prehistoric ideas, Mr. Saha. Under the circumstances there can be only one reason why he hasn't written."

She did not tell him about the endless letters she had written, loving ones, sulky ones, angry ones, imploring ones, written late at night and posted at college to avoid embarrassing questions from Arati.

"I am going to hate you for making me talk so much about myself," she said.

Arati announced dinner. Around the dinner table the conversation strayed to topics familiar to frequenters to Arati's house. Her husband, who was general manager for an electrical manufacturing company which boasted foreign collaboration, spoke feelingly about the step-motherly treatment given by the government to private industry. Other guests joined in. Mr. Saha concentrated on eating until Arati turned to him and asked him, "Tell me, how did you happen to go into politics?"

"I suppose it's a logical transition from journalism. I felt I was being dishonest, sitting in my study writing violently critical articles about government policies. I felt it was only fair to see what it was like on the other side."

"And now that you are a member of parliament, are you no longer critical of government?"

"I won't say that, but I am beginning to realize that a lot of such criticism comes from personal dissatisfaction, not from any interest in public good. Also, in a democracy people can do something about their complaints, but they are not willing to spend the time and energy. They simply want absolute freedom, but they don't want to carry the responsibility that comes with it."

Coming from anyone else, this would have sounded pompous. From him it was a simple assertion. Vicky caught his eye and gave him a smile. She saw that Arati noticed this and immediately said something to him to draw his attention back to herself. Arati didn't like to lose the limelight for a single second. It was her object in life to charm everyone, and nobody was beneath her attention. Vicky was no prude, but she thought Arati should act her age. The way she behaved was disgusting.

Everyone left the table and Vicky slipped out to the balcony. It was quiet there, but in moments the quietness became alive with the singing of mosquitoes. She felt wings brush her cheeks and slapped furiously. The stinging slap brought tears to her eyes but the mosquito got away.

"I wondered where you had disappeared to," Mr. Saha's voice said behind her.

"I hate these creatures," she said.

When she turned to him he was smiling. Even in the semi-darkness she could make out the light and dark patches of his face clearly.

"One has to be very young to hate even a mosquito so wholeheartedly," he said.

She smiled too.

"I have to leave now," he said. "I came to say goodnight."

"Oh. Goodnight."

"Vicky, will you do me the honour of dining with me tomorrow?"

She giggled and said, "I would be delighted."

He put out his hand and she saw that the back of his hand was patchy too. After a slight hesitation she gave him her hand.

The next evening when Vicky came to the living room she found Arati talking to Mr. Saha. As soon as she saw Vicky she said, "I am glad to see you have stopped acting like a broken-hearted heroine, Vicky."

Driving away in the taxi Mr. Saha said, "Your sister is a charming woman."

"Beautiful, glamorous, scintillating," said Vicky. "Don't show such poverty of language. You are a writer after all."

He was silent.

"I am sorry. I didn't mean to be nasty. I just wish she would leave me alone. I hate being treated like a little girl whose feelings are make-believe."

"Have you always lived with your sister?"

"Yes. My parents died when I was quite young. Arati and her husband are the only parents I have known."

He took her to a restaurant recommended by the friend with whom he was staying. After they had given their orders he said, "You look lovely, Vicky. I'm glad you don't adopt today's extreme fashions."

A month ago she had sported a bouffant hairstyle and white lipstick and felt very sophisticated. Just now she was glad she was in the demure phase and wore her shoulder-length hair brushed sleekly down and only a trace of pink lipstick. With him she enjoyed feeling very young.

"Tell me about yourself," he said. "What are you studying?"

"Politics and Psychology."

"What are your hobbies?"

"I swim, play tennis, dance, go to the cinema, read novels. It all sounds so silly. Let's talk about you. You are such an important person. You must be doing a lot of interesting things."

"You make me feel ancient and dull. Do I seem very old to you?"

"Not really."

"That was not a fair question. I am twice your age," he said sadly.

"Do you have a family?"

"I had a wife but we are divorced."

"Oh."

"She could not stand my leukoderma." It was easily said, without a trace of self-consciousness.

"But it's not infectious, is it?"

"No, but she found it repulsive."

"What an awful experience for you."

"It was a long time ago."

"What was she like?"

"Very beautiful. A warm and kind person."

Vicky thought, it's corny to be sentimental about a wife who divorced you for such a reason.

She said, "How did someone like you get to know my sister? You don't fit in with her usual crowd."

"We met at a party in Delhi. I happened to mention that I was coming to Bombay and she insisted that I call on her and have dinner with her."

"She likes to collect people, but usually her guest list doesn't include people like you."

"Was that intended as a criticism or a compliment?"

"A compliment of course."

"Then I must thank you."

When he left her home he thanked her and shook hands with her. She found herself thinking that the handshake probably meant more to him than a kiss to Vinod. She smiled to herself when she realized that she had not thought of Vinod all evening. She had enjoyed herself more than she had expected.

Arati was awake, reading in bed, and she called out, "My goodness, it's late, Vicky. What have you been doing?"

"We had dinner at the Sea-View and then we talked."

"All this time? What about?"

"Oh this and that. He is a nice person."

"I think he has fallen for you."

"Nonsense. He's old enough to be my father."

"It's been known to happen," Arati said drily.

He called her in the morning. "Hello Vicky, did you have a good night?"

"Yes. And you?"

"Of course. Can you give me the gift of another evening?"

"You do say the quaintest things."

"Will you? What's your programme today?"

"Nothing, except going to college."

"What time are you through?"

"Four-thirty."

"Then I shall pick you up at four-thirty."

Arati raised her eyebrows. "I hope you know what you are doing."

"Don't be so ancient. Going out with someone a couple of times doesn't mean anything."

"I know it doesn't to you."

Looking at him in the afternoon was a fresh shock. There was something exposed about the large white patches of skin in the remorseless light of day. They stopped for coffee at a place frequented by students. The night before, in the expensive dining room, with muted music and dim lights, there had been a glamour about his courtly manner, his soft voice, the extravagant compliments he had paid her. In this place he seemed pathetically old. She suddenly thought of Vinod and how much they used to laugh together.

"You are tongue-tied, Vicky. What's the matter?"

"This place is so noisy," she said irritably.

"Then if you have finished your coffee, let's get out of here."

He bought her a copy of one of his novels which had been translated into English. Then they went to Chopatty and drank coconut water and watched the sunset.

"You do seem very quiet today," he said. "Are you tired?"

"Oh no."

"Are you feeling well?"

"Quite well." She smiled at the concern in his voice. It wrapped her in a warm and secure cocoon. She considered what it would be like to be married to him. It would be nice being worshipped by him. But it might become tiresome after a while. I'd never be able to be myself, she thought.

"I am not rich," he said suddenly.

"The Sea-View is a very expensive restaurant."

"When you are alone and have nothing much to spend money on, even a small income can go a long way. But that doesn't mean I am wealthy."

"All right, but I don't know why you are telling me this."

"Don't you? Vicky, I know it's too soon, and you are too young. But in the few short hours I have spent with you, I have found reason for hope. You are a genuine and compassionate person and I have a great deal of regard for you." Vicky felt like saying, are you talking about me? He continued, "I would like to marry you. I can't offer you a lot of money, but I'll make you happy. Please don't look so disturbed. You don't have to give me an immediate answer. Just tell me if I may continue to hope."

She couldn't look at him because she felt pity for him and she was angry with him for invoking her pity.

"You haven't said anything. Have I offended you?"

"No, of course not."

"Forgive me if I have been too hasty. But I am leaving tomorrow and I couldn't go without having said this."

"I don't know how to tell you this. You were right about Vinod after all. I had a letter from him today."

"I see." He was silent for a long time and then said, "And he still loves you?"

She nodded miserably.

"And you?"

Oh stop it, please stop it, she said silently. Again she nodded.

"In that case, my dear, let me wish you happiness."

"I am sorry."

When she got home she was relieved to find that her sister was out. She was in no mood to be cross-questioned.

She undressed quickly and got into bed, but sleep eluded her. Something must be done about these mosquitoes, she thought. They don't even let you sleep.

She thought of the extraordinarily quaint things Mr. Saha said. Reason for hope. What a joke! Some men are really the limit. A girl is just friendly and they propose marriage. Twice my age, my god! And imagine living with that face for a lifetime.

Then she thought of his strange soft eyes and suddenly she was angry. He had no right to go and spoil everything, she thought.

She went to the phone, looked up his friend's number and dialled it. A woman's sleepy voice answered and Vicky asked for Mr. Saha.

"Hello, who is it?" he asked.

"Oh I am so glad to find you in. I was afraid you might have gone out," she said breathlessly.

"At midnight?" He laughed softly.

"I called to apologize."

"Apologize?" he sounded genuinely surprised.

"I haven't had a letter from Vinod. I lied to you. Will you forgive me?"

"There's nothing to forgive, Vicky."

She began to feel more and more gauche.

"I — feel flattered that you want to marry me. But I am not your sort, you know. It would never work."

"Vicky," he said. He sounded as though he were explaining a basic fact to a child. "A lady has every right to say no without offering excuses."

She tiptoed back to bed and closed her eyes. Then she turned on the bedside light and batted at mosquitoes and wondered what Mr. Saha was doing. He hadn't sounded a bit sleepy.

# THE HUNTRESS

A mosquito landed on her left forearm. This time she decided to change her tactics. She let it sit there and grow fat. When it was immobile in its satiety, she crushed it gently until the blood spilled out in a bright red stain on her arm. She looked at the stain with satisfaction, and then suddenly thought, but it's my own blood.

# THE OTHER WOMAN

It was that last cream-coloured envelope with its childish scrawl that started me on the crazy idea.

"Here's another of your paramour's letters," I said.

There had been so many of them that they had become a joke between us. Yet suddenly this particular one was more than I could stand. I felt pushed around. I had had quite enough of her childish, insistent encroachment on our life.

Satyajit was busy with his breakfast and said, "Oh."

Somehow, it was that "oh" sounding neither very casual nor really like a dismissal, that made up my mind. It would be a good idea to see her.

I thought I had left it all behind me, the wondering and the agonizing, but with the decision to confront her I began to think about her again. What was she like? Beautiful, clever, witty, attractive? Of course, all these attributes had to be thought of in the comparative. Her beauty or the lack of it was significant only in comparison with mine. There are many reasons why a wife should think of the other woman as irresistibly attractive!

I wrote to her that I would like to see her. I asked her to name the place and the day — any day after five-thirty, as I could not leave my office until five. I meant to sound like a busy, important woman in order to put our meeting in the proper perspective.

She wrote back promptly, in an exhilarant little note, that she would meet me at Emilio's on Nariman Road, at six, on the following Wednesday.

Emilio's was a teenage cafe complete with a juke box. I would not have chosen it for this meeting. I grimaced at the loud music, the loud talk, and realized that my grimace betrayed me as an outsider. Looking around at the patrons of the restaurant, formless young people, well-dressed in today's bizarre manner, self-occupied as only the young could be, I felt a fleeting envy. I could not be as young, I probably never was. What the young are today seems to preclude a specific purpose in life.

A girl waved to me from across the room. I took a quick look at her 'before going across to join her. I almost burst out laughing. This ridiculous girl and Satyajit? What he had said about her must be true after all.

She had a thin, long face, pale except for a bright orange lipstick carelessly applied. Her shoulder-length hair was straight and black. I was wrong about the lipstick. When I sat opposite her, I noticed that the lipstick followed the line of her lips faithfully, and it was her lips that were thick and uneven. Satyajit had always admired symmetry and balance, and the sculptured perfection of good bone structure.

"It was very kind of you to see me," she said. "What will you have?"

"Coffee," I said. "Cold."

"You mentioned your office. What sort of work do you do?"

"I am a medical social worker attached to the M.T. Hospital."

I was annoyed about her easy mastery of the situation. From her letters I had pictured a pretty, pathetic, broken-hearted young girl whom I could perhaps help rehabilitate.

"Let's come to the point," I said. "Much as I might enjoy it, I am not here for a nice chat over a cup of coffee. I have come to tell you that you've got to leave my husband alone. Stop pestering him with letters."

She said nothing. Her silence was self-possessed rather than rude.

"Can't you understand that he wants to have nothing to do with you? There was never anything between you, and your attempts to put a romantic construction on a casual acquaintance are ridiculous."

101

She looked up at me, her too-large eyes simulating a hurt disbelief so well that I had to admire her histrionic skill.

"Is that what he told you, that there was never anything between us?"

"Of course he did."

She smiled. A slow, sad smile.

"Naturally he would," she said. "It was a silly question. Of course, it all started casually enough. I was just someone he found interesting, someone to fill the place you had left empty. He never pretended otherwise. But then, it was out of our hands. And I just can't believe that after having meant so much to each other, he wants to end it like this."

She was full of surprises. Her eyes filled with tears. She was a young girl disappointed in her first love, pouring her heart out to me. She must be very young, I thought. Not more than eighteen or nineteen.

"What exactly did you mean to each other?"

"Surely he has talked to you about me."

"He has indeed. Would you like to hear what he said? He said that at the party at which he saw you, you looked so lonely and left out that he began talking to you. During the conversation you wangled a lunch invitation from him. After that he took you out a few times. That's all."

"A mature, gallant man giving a poor lonely girl a good time? That is the impression he would give you, isn't it?"

I was relieved to see that we were now out in the open — acknowledged enemies.

"Would you like to know what really happened? From the moment he arrived, he kept staring at me. Sometime during the evening he came and spoke to me. He told me that I had a fascinating face. 'Not beautiful in the conventional sense,' he said. 'But I hate pretty-pretty faces anyway. I would like to paint you, catch the wonderful mobility of your face.' Then he asked me to have lunch with him the next day. I was flattered, because nobody had talked to me like that before. So I accepted."

"You are lying."

"Why don't you ask him who is lying? Did he send you here to see me?"

I did not reply.

"Why can't he say his own 'no's?"

"Isn't his silence enough?" I asked.

"No. Silence is never enough."

She challenged me with her glance. Her too-large eyes and too-large mouth, her straight black hair and pale face made an arresting picture. It would offer an artist an unusual subject. I had to admit that.


Later in the day Satyajit found me in his studio and looked surprised. I was embarrassed and thought that it meant something that he should be surprised and I embarrassed in this situation. We had gradually got into the habit of travelling separate routes and taking for granted the freedom we thus gained from each other and the immunity from prying. I would have thought it very odd if I had caught him leafing through my files.

Without offering an explanation for my presence I said, "I saw your ladylove today."

"What?" he exploded.

"My dear, you seem to think that your having an affair with her was all right, but my seeing her is in bad taste."

"I did not have an affair with her. I thought we had been over all that."

I smiled.

"What's the meaning of all this smiling and insinuating? And what are you doing here anyway?"

I raised my eyebrows. "I didn't know your studio was out of bounds to me. I came to see if you were here, and then while waiting, I was just looking to see if you had done anything new."

I hadn't found what I was looking for.

"She has a fascinating face," I said. "Wonderfully mobile."

"What are you talking about?"

"Don't the words sound faintly familiar?"

"Oh you know that's just the type of thing one says to such women. It doesn't mean anything."

"Your knowledge of conversational etiquette is astounding."

"Why are you making so much of a chance remark? Sometimes when one is stuck for conversation one says anything that comes to mind to fill the pause."

"Did you also sleep with her to fill the pause?"

"Stop it. I've already told you that she meant nothing more than a casual acquaintance."

"That's not what she says."

"The hell with that she says. Are you going to believe a neurotic woman who fancies herself in love with every man who pays her the slightest attention or are you going to believe me?"

"Did you ever go to Emilio's with her?"

"What the — Yes, I did once."

"I thought so."


Considering everything, it was inevitable that we should meet again, she and I. Naturally at the same place.

"You win," I said.

"Not really," she said with that sad smile. "You see, whether he lied or not is beside the point. What matters is that he lied to spare you pain."

"I'm afraid I can't see it that way. We have never found it necessary to be dishonest with each other."

"Honesty, dishonesty," she said impatiently. "What do words matter? What matters is that somebody loves you. Whether he tells a lie or the truth to prove it doesn't matter."

"If you can believe that whatever it was, was done to prove love. Tell me, did you finally pose for him?"

"Several times."

Once long ago he had called me his inspiration. He had used me frequently as a model. But now I had a life of my own and had no time for modelling. Anyhow, it no longer appealed to me to sit for hours in one place and one position so that he could paint me. He always said that he couldn't stand an ever-present, clinging wife. A man can't have it both ways, I thought bitterly.

"Has he shown you the result?" she asked eagerly.

"I haven't asked to see it."

"He had promised to show me the finished painting," she said. Her voice had a finality, as though she no longer hoped to see it. I felt a little sorry for her.

I had wanted to ask her a lot of questions. When did they see each other? Where? How often? What did they do? Six months is a long time. Was that my only mistake? Having been away for six months? He had said I must go, it was a wonderful opportunity for me. I had not thought him capable of feeling neglected.

I used to think that if I died and he never married again, it would mean that he loved me so much that he could not imagine another woman taking my place. Sometimes I thought it could also mean that marriage had not been a sufficiently pleasant experience for him to want to repeat it.

She looked so full of her own misery that I could not thrust my questions on her. We went on drinking, she her coca-cola, I my coffee.

"I loved you too we-ell," a voice sobbed at us from the juke box.

Unexpectedly, she smiled. "You know," she said, "I am glad I met you."

"Why? Had you imagined me to be a monster who didn't understand the poor man?"

"I tried not to imagine anything," she said seriously. "I thought if I met you and had to say to myself, 'how could he have married that', it would have been awful. But if I thought of you at all, I thought of you as being quite wonderful. I thought that the only reason he picked me up was loneliness, the kind of loneliness a man feels when a wife he loves and depends on is away."

"That made everything honourable, did it?"

"There you are again. Honourable! It's just a word. I don't care about such words." She pouted a little, like a child. Her lipstick was pink today, a pale gleaming pink, the same colour as her sari. She really had a marvellous skin, a kind of luminous white without a trace of yellow or pink in it.

She was so mixed up that she would have been laughable if she had not been so pathetic. If loneliness was the only reason he had had anything to do with her, why didn't she give him up as soon as she knew I was back?

"What *do* you care about?" I asked.

"A lot of things. But they are not the same things you would care about."

"Naturally not."

She ignored my sarcasm.

"I care about love. Whenever and wherever it happens. I don't worry about the circumstances."

"Do you really mean it didn't bother you at all that he was married? I didn't figure at all in your thoughts?"

"Oh I was aware of your existence and I thought about you. I saw you among his paintings. But I didn't think our love was wrong because you existed."

"It's nice to know I didn't give anybody a bad conscience."

"Why do you want anybody to have a bad conscience? Do you think a person has a fixed arithmetical quantity of love and that in order to give it to someone he has to take it away from another?"

"You are very clever, to put it like that. But yes, reduced to simple terms, that's what it amounts to, I think."

"You are wrong. Does he love you less because of me?" With sudden impatience she said, "You are so stupid you don't even see I am the loser in this whole thing. Why do you waste your energy grudging me something that never belonged to you anyway and will no longer belong to me?"

"It's not that simple," I said. "Just because it is now convenient for him to put you in the past, I can't forget what happened."

"You can't forget and I don't want to forget," she said. Her bravado left her. "You see, he was one of the few good things that ever happened to me."

Suddenly, behind her relentless eyes I saw a dark world of deprivation, of nightmares. I didn't want to ask about it or think about it. How flippantly Satyajit had told me about her.

"You are mad," I said. "Quite mad, to talk to me like this."

This time I was not surreptitious, but I remained undisturbed until I had found what I was looking for at the bottom of a chest full of odds and ends. There were several pencil sketches, and an almost finished oil, a full-length study in vivid angry colours. Her orange mouth looked pulpy and brusied, her brilliant black eyes stared with the uncompromising look I knew so well now. And dark hair framed her dead white face. In the painting her skin looked thick and impenetrable. And her white neck rose from a mass of peacock green against which a thin white arm lay limply.

There was a sound at the door and I looked up. I thought, all is not lost yet. Now it's up to him. I didn't believe in her kind of arithmetic, and words like honesty still meant something, regardless of motives.

His look was quizzical, his smile lopsided.

"Why didn't you tell me these were what you wanted to see? I would have shown them to you," he said.

"Would you have?"

"Of course."

"Then why did you hide them in the first place? She is not the mousy, weepy thing you described, is she, Satyajit? Definitely not, I would say."

"I'd never have thought you were the kind of wife who is jealous of every female model her husband uses."

My smile strained at the corners of my mouth.

"Why did you lie about her?" I said.

"I didn't lie. But obviously I was mistaken about her. She is a clever little schemer who has succeeded in working some magic on you so that you believe her lies rather than my truth."

His voice was cool, but with a sort of intensity behind it which I knew was a symptom of anxiety.

I looked again at her hurt mouth and unflinching eyes and her dead face in the painting, and knew that I was looking in a mirror.

# A FRIEND OF THE FAMILY

The day is stretched taut between morning and evening. Usually there is a slack which I have to take up with nursing an extra cup of coffee, telephoning someone I don't particularly want to talk to, or a shopping trip to the local bazaar. We live in the suburbs, and going downtown is out of the question, as it takes half a day just to travel back and forth. I could, of course, go to the university and work on my thesis, but I am innately lazy, and there is nothing in my life which goads me to intellectual activity. I did have a go at it once. For Shekhar's benefit I registered for a Ph. D. in Psychology. But then he went away and I dropped the idea, whereupon Narendra gave his tolerant smile which he reserves for those occasions when someone does what he expects them to do.

Today is different. Shekhar is coming this evening. I was pleased at the way I came alive this morning at breakfast when Narendra read Shekhar's postcard. I had to leave the table on some pretext so that he might not see my sudden joy. Even afterwards I had to keep toning down my excitement while Narendra went on and on. He was really excited at the prospect of seeing Shekhar again. "Old Shekhar," he kept saying, shaking his head as though he couldn't believe it. "Be jolly good to see him again."

Narendra retains his British accent and British phraseology to a large extent. Shekhar, though he was in England much longer, speaks with a strong — one could say aggressively strong — Marathi accent. He constantly rags Narendra about his lack of individuality and his inferiority complex which lead him to ape the white sahib, but Narendra just smiles. That's one of the things I find endearing about him. He refuses to be baited, and when he wants to stick to a point, he refuses to argue it.

I envied Narendra this easy acknowledgment of his affection for Shekhar, though of course I am glad that we are both so fond of Shekhar, and the three of us get along so well together.

Narendra has gone to work as usual, and I have spent most of the day deciding what I should make for dinner, what I am going to wear. How will I seem to him? Will he still like my cooking? Actually it has not been such a long time — about four months? — not long enough for anything to have changed radically. Still, I wonder.

I was introduced to Shekhar during the dreary wedding reception. "Liloo, I'd like you to meet my oldest and best friend," Narendra had said. Aside from the fact that he had desisted from making the obvious wisecrack about the word oldest, he did not impress me in any way. He was one of the hundreds of people I had met that evening — the people who belonged to the clan into which, in an outdated and inadequate religious ceremony that morning, I had married.

Later when I came to know him better, as I did very soon, I found that his mind was not as undistinguished as his exterior. He called often in the evenings, did not take much persuading to stay for meals, and gave generous praise for my cooking. At first I did not quite know what to make of this frequent presence of a third person in our life, but Narendra seemed to take it for granted, and I learned to accept it. I found that Shekhar had that indescribable quality which some people have, of bringing out the best in others, of making them feel interesting. Narendra was always lively and voluble in Shekhar's presence, while otherwise he tended to be a reserved and silent companion.

They talked a lot about London, Narendra with nostalgia and Shekhar disparagingly and sarcastically, though I think they were both equally sentimental about it, not about the city but about their stay there.

Shekhar is quite a bit older than Narendra. They were next-door neighbours and Narendra had inevitably hero-worshipped Shekhar. Shekhar had not spurned the little boy's doglike devotion, with the result that they grew up to be friends. Later they were in London together when Narendra went to the London School of Economics and Shekhar, who had finished his studies years before, was postponing his return on one excuse after another, meanwhile occupying himself with doing some teaching, writing an occasional article for some paper, and participating in the Marathi language programme of the B.B.C.

They had roomed together and returned home together, much of the credit for Shekhar's return being attributed by his parents, who had given up their son for lost, to Narendra's good influence.

Looking back, I can't tell exactly when I went through the transition. There was an exact point of time, however, when I admitted to myself that such a transition had taken place, that Shekhar had come to mean something more than a friend, an occasional evening's companion, an enlivener of a life which sometimes threatened to lapse into monotony. How much more it was and where it would take me were problems which I never tackled. There was no need to. An honest self-probe could not force me to conclude that I was being unfaithful to my husband even implicitly. I still love him as much as I did when I first saw him as a prince charming in the flesh, tall, fair, with fine features and a shock of unruly hair which made women of all ages feel at once maternally and romantically inclined towards him. And if, on closer acquaintance, I have thought him to be a little too quiet, rather limited in his interests (which encompass mostly his desk job with a big drug company), and his looks a shade too delicate, his basic attraction for me has not diminished. Moreover, I could never imagine Shekhar supplanting him.

In fact, and this is not as puzzling an aspect of the whole set-up as it seemed in the beginning, the proximity of Shekhar always made me more aware of Narendra's attractiveness. I could not resist being demonstrative with him when Shekhar was there. Though Narendra was not especially responsive, he did not seem embarrassed by it. His acquiescence was enough for me. It was as though Shekhar had issued a challenge and I was telling him, look how much in love we are, how happily married.

In the earlier days of my marriage I sometimes teased Shekhar about this girl and that, and talked of finding someone smart who would do a neat job of hooking him. Once I seriously asked him why he hadn't married.

"A man loses his soul by marrying," he said.

That stung me. "Would you say Narendra has lost his soul then?"

Shekhar laughed at that, trying to make a light banter out of the conversation. "Perhaps he had no soul to lose. Or let's say, under certain circumstances it might be pleasant to lose one's soul."

He looked at me in a funny way then, sort of intensely and searchingly, and the thought flashed into my mind that he might be choosing to remain single because of me. A flattering thought. Perhaps that was the first step in the transition. Thereafter I was divided between wanting him to get married which would be a triumph for my sex, and remain a bachelor which would be a personal triumph for me. Also, as long as I was married and he was not, I could flaunt my marriedness at him and get the better of him that way.

Every time I thought of Shekhar objectively (which I invariably did in his absence), I could tell myself with relief that there was nothing in him to recommend him to a woman. A head shorter than Narendra, with a squat build which would run to fat in a few years if he didn't watch out, a square face with bushy eyebrows and thick lips black with constant smoking. And hair in his ears.

But the relief of thinking objectively about him fled when he called to say that he would call round in the evening if we were free. We were free, we always were. Narendra has no friends. He apparently doesn't need any. He has always had Shekhar, but that, I suspect, has been more out of habit for both of them than out of choice. As for me I left my old friends behind when I came to Bombay, and I have not made any new ones. The neighbours are not worth it and our get-togetherness with Narendra's colleagues and their wives are confined to formal mutual entertaining.

On receiving a call from Shekhar, I used to hurry to the kitchen to see what I could make to tempt his bachelor appetite. After watching him through a lot of meals I had come to know his likes and dislikes as well as I know Narendra's. Then when dinner time came, I artlessly asked Shekhar to share potluck with us. The potluck consisted of a carefully prepared feast which he always enjoyed.

I also tried to dress extra-carefully when he was expected. Nothing dressy or startling. Just a colour that I knew especially suited me, or a touch of perfume, or a piece of unobtrusive jewellery. It was never anything noticeable, but it made me feel specially attractive, though Shekhar rarely noticed anything I wore.

I can't tell whether Shekhar underwent a transition. He seemed to have become friendlier, more open with me before he went away. Acceptance is the word. He seemed to accept me. He drew me into a discussion deliberately which he hadn't done in the beginning. His whole attitude seemed to say that I was not included in his generally low opinion of women (which he lost not a single opportunity of expressing), that something about me set me apart. It was a partial compliment, but I was content with it.

Nothing of what I felt was expressed. There was no chance. We were never alone together except for a few seconds occasionally but that, with Narendra's return imminent, didn't count. Once in a while I thought about Shekhar dropping in unexpectedly when Narendra was away. But at the point of such a meeting my imagination failed. Or rather, it kept me at the level of a mundane exchange of words.

But Shekhar never came while Narendra was away. Narendra usually mentioned it when he was going out of town, and Shekhar made his next visit coincide with Narendra's return. I sometimes wondered why. Perhaps, in spite of his cynical attitude towards what he called conventional values, Shekhar was a loyal friend and didn't want to expose himself to my company. After all, he couldn't be entirely immune to me.

Sometimes I wondered how Shekhar came to be such great friends with my husband. Narendra is no fool, but he has an essentially provincial mind which Shekhar cannot find stimulating. On the other hand Shekhar does not seem to derive any pleasure out of making Narendra appear at a disadvantage in a contest of wits. His affection for Narendra is nothing if not genuine. So I suppose it really is a matter of habit. Perhaps even a drifter wants something to anchor him firmly to so-called normal life, and for Shekhar Narendra supplied this need.

Suddenly one day Shekhar announced that he was off to Calcutta. We were both dismayed and I asked, "Calcutta? What would anyone want to got to that dirty old city for?"

"Because one has got a job there."

Shekhar, who has a modest income from the legacy his father left him, had been a free-lance journalist and author of sorts. Now all of a sudden he decided that it was not enough to work when he felt like it.

"Somehow," he said, "it's easier to work to your full capacity when someone makes you."

"You won't like it, after being used to a life of freedom," Narendra said.

"Perhaps not. I want to find out what it's like."

"But why Calcutta? I should think there are enough newspapers and magazines which could offer you a job here."

114

"I daresay. However, I want a change of climate. This city is beginning to get on my nerves. It's too commercial, too cosmopolitan, too culture-conscious without having any real culture."

"And Calcutta is different?" I asked.

"I've heard it is. I want to see for myself."

He sounded as though he was for some reason annoyed with us, and his tirade against Bombay was really meant for us. I was struck that evening by his irritable and snappish temper. He was restless, out-of-sorts, not his usual confident, aggressive self at all. He did not stay very long and seemed genuinely sorry when he took our leave.

"Well, I hope I'll see you again soon. You youngsters have done a lot for me, but I don't want to become a fixture in your life."

"We're going to miss you," Narendra said.

"I'll miss you too, and Liloo's wonderful cooking. Keep in touch. He's a rotten correspondent, Liloo, but you'll write, won't you?"

"Of course."

I have often wondered whether he went away because of me, whether at last he was getting seriously interested in me and wanted to cure himself of it. Only that could account for his strange behaviour that evening, his sad smile at parting.

Since Narendra left this morning, I have not stopped wondering. Has Shekhar come to mean more to me than I care to admit? Supposing the feeling is mutual, what then? What are we to each other? I don't like to answer the question. The answer promises to be disturbing. For the first time Narendra comes as an intruder in my thoughts of Shekhar. Above all I wonder what Shekhar himself will be like. Has he changed? Will he still have his deadpan expression, or will I be able to read something in it? Will an impulse of any sort pass from him to me?

The moment of reckoning has finally arrived. Dinner (the weapon which I have always used to pry away his lid of self-containment and peek inside) is ready. Narendra has gone to bathe and change, and I am waiting, not really trying to read the paper I hold in my hands. A taxi stops in front of the house. Its door opens and closes, and the sounds of its driving away mask the footsteps I know are advancing to the front door.

Before I can get up, Naredra has come bounding downstairs to open the door.

"Well, at last the great man," he says.

Shekhar looks leaner and browner, more attractive than I could have thought possible. He shakes Narendra's hand. His other hand is on Narendra's shoulder and he says, "It's good to see you, my boy. Let's look at you, you have hardly changed at all." Strangely, for the bright overhead light is on, Shekhar has not seen me. I stand unmoving, savouring the quick tightening in my chest, content to put off the moment of actual meeting.

It seems as though an eternity has gone by while Shekhar and Narendra face each other. Shekhar's hand still squeezes Narendra's shoulder hard, his eyes are unnaturally bright as he gazes at Narendra unblinkly. And the quality of the tableau changes. There is no mistaking the look in Shekhar's eyes.

I've been a blind fool.

# THE HUNT

They did not see the two white caps bobbing up and down until they had crested the rise. Almost at the same moment the boys became aware of their presence. For want of anything better with which to occupy their Saturday afternoon, the boys had wandered off on the desert. Having no fixed purpose, they desultorily looked for wild berries, competed at target shooting with stones, poked at huge anthills, half-wishing that an enormous snake would crawl out of one.

The appearance of the couple had the quality of a miracle, so suddenly had they come into the line of vision. At one moment the moor had been lonely except for the wild cattle sitting still and tightly huddled together at a distance. Then suddenly, there were these people. These two strangers who did not belong here, and yet in a profound sense, belonged more than anyone else. So had the old princes, their fathers had told them, ridden and hunted deer and panthers out of existence from these parts. These two were not on horseback, but the man carried a gun in his hand. The woman was dressed in a man's clothes, and so slight and boyish was her figure that, but for her long hair drawn back in a pony tail and tied with a bright yellow ribbon, they would not have been able to tell that it was a woman.

While the two pairs took stock of each other, a fox ran out of a thicket of *bor* bushes. For a moment he looked at them standing poised on a rock, his brown fur glistening in the sun. Then he was gone.

But in that short while the man had been galvanized into activity.

"You two go around that way," he told the boys, "and get to the other side of the gully. You, Mala, should walk upstream, get down into the bed and then start back this way."

He had adopted the boys as naturally as though he had a rendezvous with them, Mala thought with quick resentment. He did not think that it encroached on their privacy. It was always his way.

She heard a complicated cry and wondered what it was. Then she realized that it must be the boys trying to imitate a bird call. She didn't know how long she had been walking, engrossed in her thoughts. Now she got down in the dry stream-bed and started working her way back. Long before she reached them, she saw them, the boys and her husband. She saw her husband take aim. She looked away from him and saw the little animal running. The next moment his movement was abruptly arrested. A brief shaft of pity made her narrow her eyes and crease her forehead. Then she walked towards the others.

The wild cattle had heard the gunshot and they grew restless. They stood up and milled about and stared hostilely at the humans. Mala could feel their hostility. People thought it against their religion to kill them and nobody dared go near enough to catch them. They wandered at will to graze on people's crops and nobody could stop them. Mala watched them, fascinated. She felt an urge to edge nearer and see what they would do. If they felt threatened, she supposed, they could harm her.

Engrossed in looking at the cattle, she had walked unwittingly into a clump of babul. A sudden prick on her heel made her aware of this. She bent down to remove the thorn from her sandalled foot, and was amused to see one of the boys also removing a thorn from his foot. She noticed for the first time that they were both barefoot. She felt ashamed of her exclamation of the pain at the prick, and even more ashamed because the place where the thorn had been now burned and her whole foot seemed to be flaming so that she was conscious only of that.

Just a thorn, she thought sadly. What must the little fox have felt just before it died? Was its whole being one blazing moment of agony?

So the hour passed. This time they got a rabbit. The feeling grew inside her that these strange boys and her husband formed a coterie and she stood on its outer fringe, unable to share either their feelings or their actions.

It is strange, she thought. We are supposed to be taking a vacation away from everything, so that we can find each other again.

"Looks like an ideal spot for rabbits," he had remarked as they drove by the moor. "Mind if I have a couple of shots?"

She had shaken her head, not really understanding why he wanted to shoot rabbit. He had jumped out of the car with the alacrity of a young boy. Full of a manifold sadness, she wandered away on her own, her mind churning with thoughts, her arms full of wildflowers which she had not even been conscious of picking.

This second honeymoon (hated phrase!) was not a good idea. People like us, she thought, whose relationship grows shallow and patterned in everyday life, become incapable of probing deeper. They are the same to each other whether they are engaged in performing the mundane duties of daily existence or alone together in a peaceful, idyllic setting. I wonder what he is thinking. But he doesn't think. He acts. He says things. He does things. But the things he says are never enough. The things he does always keep us apart. Like just now. He seems never to be aware of the under-surface currents, never to be conscious of the implications behind words and acts. Thus we end up in an eternal tangle where I cannot accept what he gives, and demand only what he is unable to give.

Glancing at her wrist watch, she saw that it was five o'clock. Time for them to be on their way if they were to reach their destination before nightfall. The sun had gone behind clouds and a light, moist breeze stirred the tender grass.

119

When she found them, he and the boys stood looking down at the loot of the day. They had bagged another rabbit since she had left them. Why should I feel a qualm, she wondered. Actually it is no different from killing mosquitoes, and I kill those by the hundreds.

"Good day's work, eh?" He hailed her.

The boys each had an empty cartridge in his hand. They turned the little metal caps round and round, feeling them with their palms. These will probably be their proudest possessions, she thought.

"Let's get going, Mala. We'll build a fire and I'll show you how to roast a rabbit." He addressed her with tender enthusiasm, singling her out as though only she was there. He did not think of asking her where she had been. He did not insist that she share his interest in the hunt. He did not seek to possess her totally. Yet she felt that all the time she had been away from him, she had been constantly present in his thoughts. She felt humble.

Then she thought of the boys. What was to be done with them? Should they be paid? Just dismissing them seemed abrupt and rude.

"I'll give you a rabbit's ear each, and then you run back home," he said.

We have come a long way from the town, she thought. Shouldn't we offer them a lift back? But the boys were already running towards the town, their treasures clutched tight in their hands.

He had got rid of the boys as quickly and easily as he had adopted them. Yet it was not as if he had merely used them. The boys might have accepted money, but they couldn't have thrilled to the touch of money the way they had to the touch of the hard metal and the soft rabbit's ear, symbols of the exciting afternoon. And he had known this with certainty while she had fumbled embarrassedly for a way to dismiss them.

"Let me put your flowers on the back seat," he said. "They won't last, but they are beautiful. They don't last even if you put them in water, and they won't be civilized. I think that is their charm. When I was a little boy I used to uproot the little plants and bring them to our garden. But however well I cared for them, they never survived."

This is not rediscovering, Mala thought. I had never known the child who tenderly transplanted wild flowers, only to be disappointed when they died, the young man who revelled in hunting for the sheer excitement of the sport regardless of what the prey was. I did not know the man who thought wild flowers were beautiful, and did not consider it below his manly dignity to say so. I had never cared to know. Nor had I ever realized his art in dealing with people. He feels quick sympathy with all human beings. He is kind and large-hearted without becoming involved. Deep in the centre of his being there is no room for multitudes. That is occupied only by a few who mean something to him, who stay there always, no matter where he is or what he is doing. And I am one of them. If I have enough faith in this love, I may learn then not to demand proof of it in the trivial, overt acts and expressions for which it has neither time nor need.

# TURNING POINTS

Jagdish and I had a senseless quarrel. For years we had had a sort of a truce. At first it was full of a stiff and cold politeness which indicated that we hoped for something different. Then it gradually deteriorated into a casual amity which meant that we had admitted the end of a relationship. And then suddenly came the quarrel.

When I arrived at the lab that morning, I found a message waiting for me that he wanted to see me as soon as I came in. He was beaming.

"Start packing. You are going to New York."

I had submitted a paper on the manufacture of a cheap food supplement which would contain all the ingredients which a pregnant woman's diet should have. What he was telling me meant that my paper had been selected to be read at the annual meeting of the International Association for Applied Nutrition, and that I was getting an all-expense-paid trip to New York for the purpose.

"And I have some more news for you," he said before I could respond suitably to his announcement. "You are being offered a guest lectureship for six months at the Institute for Applied Nutrition."

I sat down slowly and deliberately, knowing that he would interpret this to mean that I did not receive the news without reservations.

"Well," he said.

"I can't go."

"What do you mean you can't go?"

"Just that I can't go."

"Then why the hell did you submit the paper? You must have had an idea that your paper would be selected. You are aware of your standing in the field of applied nutrition."

"At the time I submitted the paper I didn't know anything about the lectureship. Going to the conference is one thing, spending six months abroad is quite another."

"Are you really telling me that you won't go?"

"Yes. I am sorry."

"I suppose you have a good enough reason for turning it down."

"Yes, though you won't think it a good enough reason."

And so we finally quarrelled about what we had probably wanted to quarrel about all along. Bichu. I told him that I could not leave Bichu alone to shift for himself for six months. It was his final year in medical college, and it just wouldn't be fair to him, specially as we did not have a full-time servant who could keep house for him, or relatives with whom he could stay for the duration.

"And you talk of women's lib," Jagdish said. "No man would ruin his career for a silly reason like that."

"That's because men are blindly devoted to their work. They have no sense of proportion."

"You are so blindly devoted to your precious son that you have no right to even talk about a sense of proportion. Nobody would think, to hear you, that he was a twenty-three-year-old man perfectly able to take care of himself if you'd only let him. Does it occur to you that you are doing him a disservice by being so protective?"

"I didn't ask your advice about him. And anyway, you can't seriously tell me that my whole career depends on whether I attend this stupid conference or not."

"Anything you don't think important is stupid. If you think it's stupid why did you submit a paper for it?"

"Don't shout."

"I'll shout if I want to. You've no right to tell me what to do or what not to do. I could throw you out for this, do you know that? Then where will your career be? And don't tell me you can get another job. You couldn't in a hundred years get a job just like this."

He was right. It would be practically impossible to find another job doing exactly what I wanted to do, working with a man like him who admitted the value of my work and went out of his way to take as much of the burden of administrative work off my shoulders as he could. All the same, I didn't like him to say it, to use it as an argument.

I said, "Are you blackmailing me?"

Suddenly the swollen veins on his forehead subsided, the anger drained out of his eyes to be replaced by pain. We looked at each other in the sudden calm and felt a terrible need for physical contact. Across the table our hands travelled towards each other, met and clung, and the touch had far greater consent than many moments of greater intimacy which we had shared.

"I am sorry," he said. His voice was almost impersonal. "Do what you think is best, but don't take the final decision now." He held up his other hand. "No, don't say anything more. Don't make me say things I'll regret later. We'll leave this open for a couple of days. Think it over and let me know what you decide on Monday."

His voice told me that he knew the waiting was merely a formality. I nodded and left him.

Even though I had expected anger, the full force of it left me shaken, and also exhilarated that he still cared so deeply. But the exhilaration was followed by anger as I realized that his caring gave me a responsibility which I did not want. Why must I arrange my life always according to what I felt I owed to others? The anger stopped me from thinking about the pain which I had not seen in his eyes for a long time, not since the time years ago when he asked me to marry him and I said no. I had wished that it could be otherwise, because I had loved him. I still loved him in a muted non-urgent way. But I had to make a choice, and the choice clearly had to be in Bichu's favour. Suppose Jagdish was not the sort of father Bichu needed. Suppose they could not get along and this created emotional problems for Bichu, put a wedge between us during the critical years when he needed me most, I would never stop blaming myself. So I had made my choice, and I had to stick to it. I owed nothing to Jagdish.

When I came home that afternoon, Bichu was already there. There was a girl with him, which was not unusual, as I had always seen to it that he felt free to bring his friends home. I did not feel in a particularly sociable mood and acknowledged the introduction and her greeting with only superficial attention. Then some sixth sense made me look at Bichu. He was watching me anxiously, which told me that this was a special girl. She was the girl I had thought about so often, without thinking about specific characteristics. Now the outline was filled in. Name: Sarita, a currently fashionable one. Face: insipidly pretty. No character. Oh now, I told myself, let us not be catty. Just say she is pretty. No qualifications.

I looked more closely at her as we sat down and indulged in the usual senseless casual exchange reserved for such occasions. She had a simpering way of talking which I found irritating. She was dressed in a very brief blouse which showed most of her smooth back, and a sari worn below the waist which showed the young curves beneath. Her hair was longer than shoulder length, loose down her back. Her eyes were heavily made up to look slanting, and her lips had the greenish-blue gloss which makes me think of a dead body. The effect, I had to admit, was not unattractive, but the effort and the time it involved must have been considerable. Obviously she had nothing more important to do than making herself pretty. I stopped myself. I was being catty again.

I said, "Bichu, why don't you get us all some coffee?"

Sarita's plucked and shaped eyebrows went up slightly. She said prettily, "I'll make it." She followed him to the kitchen.

125

How quaint and wifely her outrage. When there is a woman around, why should the man of the house have to work in the kitchen? An attitude which Bichu — any man — must find appealing, and which I had tried to train him away from. I wanted him to believe, as I believed, that there is no such thing as man's work and woman's work. I wondered what Sarita would think if she knew that I had asked him to make the coffee with the specific intention of calling forth this outdated response from her.

Since I was left alone in the living room I went to have a wash. Next to the girl I felt dishevelled and jaded after a day of work, and after the unresolved conflict with Jagdish. I washed my face with plenty of soap, and immediately felt the skin tighten with dryness. Everything about me felt dry. I rubbed some cold cream on my face, combed my hair, considered and abandoned the idea of changing my sari. Why should I feel the need to compete with this girl? I had so much more going for me. Except youth and beauty, I thought. And at a certain age, or perhaps at any age, that's what matters most to a man. Maybe Jagdish no longer wants me, maybe what he loves now is just a memory of what I used to be.

Bichu called out that the coffee was ready. Before I stepped out of my room, I heard Sarita say, "Isn't it unfair when parents let children get stuck with silly baby names?" So she had already begun to wage war.

His name is Vishwas, but when he was a toddler, if anyone asked him what his name was, he said Bichu, and that's what we began calling him. I had never thought it ranked with silly names like Baby and Bal, and I have always thought that the name suits him, expresses what he is, boyish, spontaneous, open.

I joined them, picked up my cup and started sipping from it. Bichu and Sarita filled the uneasy silence with bright chatter about inconsequential things. Sarita's roommate who back-combed her hair and was losing it, the hero of a movie they had seen, about whose looks they squabbled good-naturedly, the elections in her college. Could anyone really be so mindless? At her age I had so many more interesting, important things to talk about.

"What are you studying?" I asked her.

"I am in my third year B.A."

"What subject?"

"Economics."

"What do you plan to do after your B.A.?"

Bichu had been getting uncomfortable during this exchange. Before she could reply to my last question he quickly said, "Let her pass her exam first, then she can decide."

"But you must have some idea," I persisted, still looking at her.

"I haven't really thought about it."

Bichu said flippantly, "Everyone doesn't have to think and plan their life from the time they are in high school. Also everyone doesn't have to think in terms of a career."

"Every woman, you mean."

"Yes. I mean, it's all right talking about equality of the sexes, but you can't get away from the fact that their roles have to be different. A woman can pull her weight keeping house, bringing up children. I mean, that can be a legitimate career."

"I suppose so," I said, dazed.

Can it be called love when it has the power to turn a man's ideas, attitudes, his mind completely topsy-turvy, tear down what has taken years to build?

If he had to marry, why couldn't he at least pick — . I pulled myself up sharply. If. What do you mean if? Had you really considered the possibility that he might never marry? No, I said.

In connection with other women, I had always used the facile psychological cliches to explain why they could not get along with their daughters-in-law. Now was I going to be reduced to the lowest common denominator?

If only she were more worthy of him —

No, that's not true. If she were perfection itself, you still would not have relinquished him to her with grace. In fact a part of me was pleased that she was what she was. Ultimately sometime, even though Bichu might not admit it, he would realize that I was the better person.

So there I was. All the more vulnerable now because I had thought myself invulnerable. I had thought, after all, I am not like other women. I have my work. My life does not revolve completely around Bichu. I will give him my blessings when he finds a wife.

"Well, I had better be going," Sarita said, getting up.

Bichu said, "I'll see you to the hostel. It's late."

It was only seven-thirty, but she was helpless, appealingly feminine and precious, and could not be allowed to go alone.

He put his arm around her waist. It occurred to me that these two had known each other a long time. They were easy, natural together. Anger throbbed at my temples. Why had Bichu been so sneaky? Why hadn't he ever mentioned her? He had probably brought her here often, used my house for their clandestine meetings.

The image of his hand on her bare skin remained with me. How intimate were they? I thought of his body being awakened to new sensations, then sated. I felt a deep pain. A body gets used to being sated. After Bichu's father died, I had spent night after night aware of nothing but my tortured nerves straining for something they would never find. At that time, desperately caught in my protean anguish, I had wondered why, if one of them had to die, it couldn't be Bichu. I was as old then as Bichu is now. So what, I thought. Am I grudging him something which I was deprived of through no fault of his?

And what about Jagdish? Why, after discovering my own capacity for reawakening, had I forced myself to face frustration again?

It was time to take myself in hand. If I had made any sacrifices for Bichu, it was not because he asked me to make them. How could I, when my convictions about such things had always been clear-cut, now think in terms of returns, of gratitude, for something I had done for my own gratification?

During dinner Bichu asked, "What do you think of her?"

I was prepared for the question. "She is very nice." Just that. I was learning the tactics of this particular kind of warfare.

"What would you say if I told you I want to marry her?" he asked as though springing a surprise on me.

"I would say, give it enough time to make sure that she is someone you can respect, then go ahead."

"We've known each other long enough. Oh I know you are worried because she seems unambitious, but everyone can't be brilliant like you, you know. And in the end, if we love each other enough, nothing else will matter."

After a few mouthfuls he said, "We would like to get married as soon as possible."

"How soon is that?"

"How does this December sound to you? Her parents will be here then."

"But Bichu, you are still in college. Why not wait until you finish?"

"What's the point in waiting once we have decided to marry?"

Well, one point was that he would then be able to support a wife. Was it possible that Bichu was being irresponsible enough to expect me to support both of them for perhaps years to come? Was he so helpless in the face of his own feelings that he could not wait to marry until he could stand on his own feet? But saying all this to him was not going to fit in with the strategy I must follow if I wanted to save myself a small space in his life. This devious sparring had never been part of our relationship, and I hated Sarita for making it necessary. I recoiled at the prospect of working for them and keeping house

129

for them and hating every minute of it and not being able to show it.

I said, "No point, I suppose, if you have made up your mind. Only I won't be here."

"What do you mean you won't be here?"

The sudden explosion of his voice was soothing to me. I explained what I meant.

"Oh." He didn't seem to know what his reaction should be.

"Well, it doesn't really matter, does it?" I said.

"I suppose not."

I scraped up the faint regret in his voice and smiled. I was glad I had said it out loud as soon as I had thought of it, and not left myself a way out. I simply could not let myself face the worst in myself. And the only way to prevent it was running away.

I did not wait till Monday. I told Jagdish the next morning that I had changed my mind. He was drafting a letter which he held out to me. It said that I regretted that I could not be present at the conference for reasons of ill health, and that, as he was going to be present anyway, and was familiar with my work, he hoped it would be acceptable for him to read my paper.

"I didn't know you were going," I said. But of course I should have known. I should have known that his violence was the violence of personal disappointment. The syndrome that I called love seemed to have lowered instead of heightening my sensitivity to the person I claimed to love.

"Now that you know, would you like to change your mind again?" he asked quietly.

I shook my head. He did not smile, but the tight lines of his face relaxed. I lowered my eyes. If there was anything in them to read, I did not want him to read it. I was merely running away. Where I stopped and how might ultimately depend on him. But for the time being I had no right to hope, or let him hope, since my choice had not been governed by his needs.

# NIGHT SOUNDS

*Tuesday*

I wonder how much of what we are, what we feel and do, depends on our body chemistry. I wonder if, when we think we are reacting to outside stimuli, we are only reacting to our insides. Two hours ago, riding in the tonga with my feet resting on my fat suitcase and my knees jutting ridiculously out in front of me, with a long tiring train and bus journey behind me and a bone-rattling two-mile tonga ride ahead of me, I felt unaccountably elated, free. The moon, its sullen orange orb flattened on one side, had just risen above the horizon, and watching it I thought that it was symbolic. And now two hours later, with the moon bright and high in the sky, and the warmth and peace of this place around me, instead of feeling happy and drowsy, I am restless and wide awake. It's not the wakefulness I mind — I don't get hysterical over loss of sleep — it's this sense of something not quite in place, a sense almost of depression, alien to my nature, that troubles me, and is, I console myself, probably due only to fatigue.

I heard them talking after Mummy left me — so Daddy had been awake — and now they are silent, asleep, my wise parents who knew exactly what they wanted in life, and exactly how to get it.

Mummy said when she opened the door, "You! What are you doing here? Why didn't you let us know? We could have sent someone to the bus stand."

She looked tussled, grumpy and adorable, and I laughed.

"I wanted to give you a surprise."

"Would you like something to eat? I'll make your bed. You will have to sleep in the living room. I've converted the spare room into a study."

"Don't bother please, Mummy. I know where everything is."

"Well then, if you are sure you don't want anything, I'll go back to bed."

On the point of turning away she stopped. "What brings you here so suddenly?"

"I've come to stay."

"What do you mean?"

I gave a little laugh. "I have decided to come and look after you in your old age."

She said wryly, "I heard it a little differently the last time you spoke on the subject."

I put my arms around her. "Oh Mummy, that was long ago and I was an irresponsible adolescent and Daddy had got me angry."

She extricated herself gently and said, "Well, we'll talk about it tomorrow."

She vanished into her dark bedroom. I made myself some cocoa and a sandwich out of homemade bread. I made up a bed on the living room divan. But now I find I cannot sleep. Certainly 11 p.m. is not a time for enthusiastic welcomes, and I mustn't feel neglected, but I keep an ear cocked towards their bedroom, hoping she will find herself unable to sleep and come out to talk to me. I would have thought we had come closer during the past two years, enough at least for her to feel curious about me. Does she still hold that long ago defiance against me?

When Daddy left Bombay he was an angry and bitter man. A "friend" had swindled him out of a substantial sum of money, he had been superseded in his job because he had displeased the wrong person, a sister to whom he had been particularly close had been murdered along with her husband and a baby in her flat by their servant. It was not surprising that he simply wanted to get away from Bombay, as far away as possible in every way. He had, of course, taken for granted that I would go with them. He assured me that there was a perfectly good college in Sangvi, moderately big town some twenty-five miles from where they would live. I flatly refused. He raged and threatened.

"You are free to go and bury yourself in that hole, but you have no right to force me to resign from the world," I said.

"Where will you stay?" Mummy said.

"There are hostels."

"I have heard of such awful conditions in hostels."

I shrugged. "You leave me no choice."

Daddy roared, "I refuse to support you if you go on living in Bombay."

"All right," I said with a nonchalance I was far from feeling. "I'll look for a job. I am a major, so I cannot claim support from you, but just be sure that you don't expect me to look after you in your old age."

Mummy had finally prevailed upon him to continue to support me by more or less convincing him, I think, that leaving me to my own devices would be forcing me into a life of sin. I kept an account of every paisa Daddy paid me and paid it back later. I don't think he has ever forgiven me that.

Many years later I finally accepted one of Mummy's imploring invitations to visit them. I found Daddy much more even-tempered, more tolerant. Perhaps he did not feel as responsible for a twenty-five-year-old as he had for an eighteen-year-old. Perhaps he had stopped caring about me. It took me a couple of years of frequent visits to establish what could be termed friendly communication with him. Even then my privileges were strictly circumscribed. When I asked if sometimes I could bring along a friend just for the weekend, Daddy said, "Chitra, you are our daughter and this is your home whenever you want to come here, for however long you want to stay. But I don't want you to use this as a sightseeing spot for your city friends. I hope you will respect our privacy to that extent."

I was furious with him but now I am glad that he has kept this place out of the reach of old friends. I feel as though I were inside his skin. Without the help of a series of traumas I have arrived at the same place where he found himself seven years ago. I only wish there was some way of telling him this. Maybe some day I will.

*Wednesday*

Mummy started questioning me in earnest this morning. Daddy said, "I'll leave you to thrash it out."

"What is there to thrash out?" But neither of them answered my question. Daddy went out whistling. He was dressed, as usual, in khaki pants and a colourful checked shirt. His face is lined and tanned and he is quite proud of this. A few years ago he dressed in formal clothes and sat in an air-conditioned office nursing an ulcer and never whistled.

"Now let's hear what this is all about," Mummy said, very crisp and businesslike.

"It's about my having given up one sort of life for another."

"What about your job?"

"I've given it up."

"No! Have you really?"

"Well, I've taken a month's leave with the understanding that if they hear nothing from me before the month is over, they take it as a resignation."

She looked relieved. I thought with amusement of my meeting with my immediate superior.

He had said, "I must admit I am surprised, and that's putting it mildly. A person with your talents, in a job so well suited to them, with an almost unlimited scope for rising up the ladder in the organization or out of it! What are you doing leaving all this? If you are in any way dissatisfied with the conditions of work —"

"I am not."

"Then what is it?"

I could have said that I was going to do the things I had always wanted to do. Paint for instance. I'd much rather paint that plan a campaign to sell women the idea that they would achieve desirability if they used a certain brand of talcum powder. But deriding a job that you have enjoyed doing is a cheap trick. And it wouldn't even be true. Certainly there were times when I felt that the things I was doing were stupid. But when I was behind the door which bore the legend Rashmi Advertising Pvt. Ltd., sitting at the desk labelled Director, Art Department, I was doing a job I enjoyed doing.

When he saw that I couldn't offer him a justification for what I was doing, he smiled paternally and said, "I think all you need is a long holiday. Tell you what, I'll sanction you a month's leave, though God knows how I'm going to be able to spare you. You go and live on this farm of yours. In a month if you feel you have worked whatever it is out of your system, we will welcome you back. If not —" He had made a rueful face and shrugged, but his voice said that he was absolutely certain that it would work out his way.

Mummy said, "Don't you like your job any longer?"

"I like it fine."

"You were very enthusiastic the last time I saw you."

"I said I like it."

"Then what is it?"

I tried. "I have begun to feel that there is something unreal about my life. It is derived, parasitical."

"What do you mean? You earn your own living."

"It's the way I earn it. Helping sell things — not even sell them myself — which somebody else has manufactured. That's twice removed from a primary activity."

Mummy shook her head. "You are being silly." She was right in a way. As civilization progresses, an endless array of people have to be engaged in secondary activities. The point was that I had wearied of my life first and then tried to find a reason for it (because everything must have a reason) and could not find a plausible sounding one.

Throughout the day Mummy continued to throw out questions and doubts. She kept saying she didn't want me to make a terrible mistake.

I said, "You didn't have any such misgivings when Daddy gave up his job and came here."

"What's right for one person may not be for another. Your father came originally from a village. His people have been farmers in these parts for generations."

"And he has it in his blood? You don't really believe that, do you?"

It appeared that she did believe it. And when I pointed out that his people were my people too, she told me I was born and brought up in Bombay, that essentially I was a city person, that I couldn't be happy living here forever. When I started arguing this she said, "Let's not talk about it any more. Now that you are here why don't you just relax and rest and forget about everything else? And eat more. You are too skinny."

So she has taken refuge behind a mother's classical concern for a child — her health.

*Thursday*

Today Mummy finally got around to asking the question, "What about Anand?"

Anand was a name I had dropped accidentally long ago while narrating something and Mummy had pounced on it because it was the only name I had ever let drop, and got me to admit that all right, I was interested in him.

"That's off."

"So that's why this sudden fit of *vairagya*!" She was happy to have found some reasonable explanation for my behaviour.

"Mummy, you know there never was anything in it."

"Wasn't there?"

"Absolutely not."

She sighed. "I really should have arranged a marriage for you when you were twenty. Your aunt was right. I shirked my responsibility."

"You don't really believe that rot."

"Well, it seems to me I should have done something." Then an idea struck her. "Would you like me to invite Anand here for a visit?"

"Good God no, what will I do with him?"

"There must be someone else then that you would like to invite."

"There isn't anyone."

"It's not natural for a beautiful intelligent girl like you not to be able to meet someone who wants to marry her."

"I have met plenty who wanted to marry me, but none I wanted to marry."

"You have — nothing against men, do you?"

I said, laughing at her struggle to arrange the world into neat little patterns, "No, I have nothing against men. Just to reassure you, I enjoyed a very satisfactory sexual relationship with Anand."

She gasped. "Then why?"

"You don't marry someone just because you have a satisfactory sexual relationship with him, do you?"

*Friday*

Last night I dreamed of Anand. I call the man in my dream Anand because I have a vague feeling that I could identify him. But even in the dream it was not possible to identify him with any certainty. He was faceless, possibly a conglomerate. The dream troubles me because I cannot recall its substance.

Anand and I parted amicably some weeks ago. On our last morning together he said, on waking, "You know Chitra, you are the only woman I know who looks beautiful all the time, even early in the morning." I gave a lazy smile and swung my legs to the floor in a graceful arc and said, "Coffee, darling?" Darling was a good contentless word that served in the place of a name. I thought how much sweeter his words would sound if I looked haggard and frowsy and were dressed in old comfortable pajamas. The thing was, I did look haggard and frowsy in the morning, but I had, as I always did when I was with him, got up a few minutes earlier and got back into bed after making myself presentable. Anand was not the man to whom I could appear anything but perfect, and I knew also that I would never meet such a man. That we parted amicably proved that he was not the man. As far as I was concerned, the quest was over. I could not, would not, make the effort again, and I felt relieved when I took this decision, free of an unwanted burden.

*Sunday*

I have begun to feel happy here. I liked the place before because it offered a perfect escape. Now I am involved in its life, its rhythm. Here one does things that must be done. Cows and buffaloes have to be milked, chickens have to be fed, plots of wheat must be fertilized and irrigated (the people here quaintly call it feeding a crop. To them a crop is as much a living thing as a bullock or a chicken), vegetables must be harvested. And yet this necessity is not the necessity of meeting deadlines, keeping appointments, following a timetable.

Today we harvested cabbages and eggplant and tomatoes for the market. I helped in the harvest and my hands got badly pricked by the eggplant spines and then itched when the tomato leaves stained them, but I stuck to it. The women made gentle fun of me because I was so slow. I felt that the different colours and textures of the vegetables, their bright dewy look against the yellow-brown earth and green foliage, the movement of hands, arms, legs as the men and women work — all this has some immediate connection with a basic part of one's being. When I said so, Mummy mildly sneered. She goes about her work with concentration and seems offended if I talk about enjoyment, significance. Such concepts are extraneous to her scheme. She takes all this very seriously, makes a point of telling me that she and Daddy didn't come here just for fun. They have to make the farm pay and it's hard work. And yet she seems infused with a deep contentment which I envy and aspire to.

Daddy took the vegetables to the weekly market twenty-five miles away and brought back cooking oil, pulses, spices, kerosene — a miscellany of items which Mummy unpacked with the delight of a child who expects to come upon a sudden treasure. And she did. There was, hidden among the mundane necessities, a box of *pedhas* to pamper her sweet tooth. I looked at her closely, and saw that her pleasure at receiving the present was genuine, or else very well faked.

It is late at night now and I lie in bed (still on my divan, Mummy has not said anything about reconverting the study into a bedroom), identifying the night sounds. One of the buffaloes stamps in her pen. A cricket shrills outside my window. A bullock cart passes on the road, making a great clatter with its wooden wheels. And an owl hoots a query. Hoo?

There is a great sense of peace in living in this warm world, connected with the bigger world with only tenuous threads. Daddy chose this place — two miles even from the nearest village — to discourage any but the most motivated visitors.

The dirt road which goes by the farm is surfaced by ankle-deep dust which turns into ankle-deep mud when it rains, and until it dries, it is impassable for anything but a bullock cart.

The owl hoots again and I smile, stopping my writing to peer into the darkness which is unrelieved by street lights and neon signs.

*Wednesday*

Every time Mummy sees me at loose ends she says, "Bored, Chitra?" and I say without emphasis, "Of course not."

I have been here a week but I still feel her watching me. While I knead the bread dough, churn the buttermilk, boil the butter for making ghee, all under her supervision because I am still inept — she sometimes grumbles that my doing these things means more work for her than her doing them herself — she watches me. Sometimes without warning she asks a question.

"Don't you find doing these chores tiresome?"

"Not at all."

"After your interesting life in Bombay you must think life is pretty dull here."

I have a mad flight of imagination in which I think that all these questions she is really asking herself, then I look at her bland face and shake the thought off.

I say, "I don't want excitement, I want peace."

"How long will you be satisfied with peace?"

"Forever."

I think that she has begun to like having me around. I am company for her in the way people on the farm cannot be. She even likes arguing with me for the sake of conversation. Daddy seems to spend very little time with her, and I try to remember whether it was always so, but cannot. I am happy to feel this bond, made up strand by strand with shared work and talk, growing between us. One day I said that one's only valid relationship is with one's mother, and she snorted.

"You don't know what you are talking about. One day you will get married, then I'll come and ask you about valid relationships."

"I am not going to marry, Mummy."

"Then what are you going to do? Live here for the rest of your life?"

I said calmly, "That's what I keep telling you."

I wish she would stop trying to test my good faith, springing these questions on me, hoping to catch me unawares. I wish she would believe me when I tell her that I am perfectly happy here, not bored or restless or anything else. I feel like a criminal whom nobody will believe reformed.

*Sunday*

The first half-hour after getting here I spent in becoming re-acquainted with the place, the feel of it. Then I had a bath to wash the dust of the long journey off my skin and an icy coke to wash my dust-parched throat. The ecstasy as it goes tingling down! Perhaps it was an indication of something, as Mummy would say, that I had left the refrigerator running. I got on the phone.

"Darling, how marvellous. Where have you been?"

"On a holiday."

"Lucky you, to be able to get away like that. Where did you go?"

"I'll tell you about it. Listen, I want to throw a homecoming party. Can you come? Tomorrow at nine."

"But day after tomorrow is a working day."

"So what? I am in a celebrating mood."

"Oh all right."

As I put down the receiver, I thought of yesterday's farce. It would make a delicious story to tell the crowd tomorrow. "My dears, a man to 'look' at me, can you beat that for sheer comedy? Parents are honestly the outer limit. Just try and think of me married, will you?"

Yesterday at breakfast Daddy announced that we were having a visitor.

"A visitor? In this place?"

For one wild moment I thought that it was Anand, that somehow Mummy had contrived to get in touch with him. But what could she have possibly said to lure him there? But it turned out to be the son of the chairman of a nearby sugar factory. He had just returned from abroad after a business-management course. Mummy and Daddy, who never had guests, entertained in style, and contrived to leave me alone with him for half an hour, during which period I was supposed to dazzle him into proposing marriage.

After he left Mummy asked me, "What did you think of him?"

"He is all right. A bit of a boob, but all right."

Daddy said, "I think he is a very fine young man. I had a chance to talk to him and he has some really sound ideas."

"I don't doubt it. I just wish you'd give it up."

Mummy said, "Well, if you don't like him, there's no harm. There are other men."

It was not really in character for her to show this desperate need of Indian mothers to see their daughters married, and I wondered, as I lay in bed last night, whether she had taken on the colour of the countryside she lived in. I heard Daddy and Mummy talking next door. Their voices were low and I couldn't distinguish the words. Then I heard a loud whisper, "Pratap, for heaven's sake, Chitra is in the next room," and Daddy saying clearly, "Chitra is always going to be in the next room," and Mummy again in a louder whisper, "Sh!"

The next morning while I was packing Mummy came in and asked me what I was doing.

I said, "If Daddy can run me to the bus stand in the van, it will save me a tonga ride. Then I can take the early bus and be in Bombay by this evening. I can have a good night's sleep before starting work in the morning."

"But —"

"You are right. This was fun for a while, but I am not cut out for this sort of life really. I am a city person at heart."

# A WORLD OF YOUR OWN

The noise and movement of buses rumbling in and out of the terminus, more than anything else, seemed to set the evening mood of Poona. People were everywhere, hurrying, talking, pushing and being pushed. Susan found it unnerving and thought it ironical that she should come to this country twice on a personal quest. Her father would probably have said that she had come for the wrong reason, both times. Right or wrong, she was here. After fighting a battle with her self-respect, she had come to the conclusion that she had travelled to the point where only self-preservation had relevance. And self-preservation meant Guru.

Just as she thought of him, she saw him coming down the sidewalk towards her. This was bound to happen sometime. In spite of its big-city airs, Poona was still small enough for people to run into each other accidentally. She was glad that their meeting had happened this way.

He said, "Susie? No, it can't be!"

In her fantasies there had been delighted disbelief on his face and he had swept her into his arms, reluctant to let her go now that he had found her again. This plot was awful, she knew, like the plots of all the impossibly romantic novels which she greedily read.

Actually there was only amused surprise on his face as he stood about three feet away from her and said, "Susie? No, it can't be!"

She laughed.

"What are you doing here?"

His casual inquiry piqued her.

"I have as much right to be here as you do," she said, her voice coming out testy and bad-tempered.

"Of course. When did you get back?"

"A week ago."

"Just like that!"

"Why not?" Now she could manage her voice better.

He was looking at her.

"Susie, what have you done to yourself?"

"I wondered when you would get around to asking."

"Well, you have — changed."

She laughed again. "What you really mean is, I've become fat and middle-aged."

She dared him to deny it. He didn't.

He seemed about to make some parting remark when she said quickly, "If you have time, why don't we go get ourselves some coffee and talk?"

"Why not?"

In the crowded restaurant he raised his voice slightly and said, "What are you doing here?"

"I am supposed to be writing a novel."

"I read your last one."

"I made sure you would," she said wryly.

"It was good. Really. Not that I am a reliable critic. But I liked it."

"Thank you."

"Are you here on your own now?"

"No, I have a fellowship."

"Still wangling fellowships, I see. Why? As I recall, you were not wildly in love with this country the last time you were here."

The waiter, a young boy with a dirty duster thrown across his shoulder, set two cups of coffee down so hard on the table that some of the coffee sloped into the saucers. This irritated her. She could never understand how Guru, so meticulous himself, could stand this kind of sloppiness. Sipping the sweet milky coffee, it was her turn to look at him.

He had changed quite a bit, aged. The smooth boyish contours of his face had given way to a slightly fleshy neck and jaw, and he had a rougher skin and a turned-down mouth which was somehow very appealing. His eyes had a little yellow in them and they seemed less green and less brilliant.

"What's the verdict?" he said.

"How old are you, Guru?"

"Forty-two. Has my age begun to show?"

"You are as attractive as ever."

With the kind of looks which would have made any other man vain, he had never known how to receive compliments gracefully.

Ignoring her remark he said, "What brings you here, really?"

His persistence made her wonder briefly whether he sensed the real reason, and wanted to make her say it. In her more desperate moments she had thought she would throw herself on his mercy and say, Guru, I need your help, that's why I have come back. I am at a dead end, and don't know where to go from here.

But now she could not see herself doing that.

She said, "I told you. I have a fellowship to complete a novel."

"That only explains the mechanics of your coming. Not the reason."

She shrugged. "It can serve as a reason too."

"Well, it's nice to see you back. How long are you going to stay?"

"A year. Maybe more. It depends."

"I hope I'll see something of you. Now I'm afraid I've got to run."

Following him with her eyes, she suddenly caught a glimpse of herself in one of the mirrors set at a crazy angle high up on the wall of the restaurant. An imposing body and a ridiculous face. A narrow mouth and deepset eyes hidden in fat cheeks. Once she had asked Guru what he saw in her and he had said, "You are plump and pretty and fun to be with. You can enjoy life without worrying about tomorrow."

It was a lifetime ago, and the day on which he said it had been perfect until that moment.

Susan held her father responsible for the way life had treated her, for, if it had not been for him, she would not have left India; or, having left, come back. She had always laughed at spiritual quests, especially ones which took you East. But, behind the express purpose of visiting the place where her father had lived and worked, was the idea that something in this country had kept hold of him until he died. She wanted to look for that something and see if it would serve her.

She was born in India. When she was three her mother died. Judging himself incapable of caring for so small a child, her father had sent her to her mother's parents. He visited her once every two or three years. In the beginning it was she who was shy of him, because she saw him so infrequently. Later as she grew up and wanted to establish real communication with him, it was he who withdrew from her. His visits became transparently duty visits, his letters in response to hers, dry and disappointing. It seemed to her that they were not even close enough for her to express the resentment she felt. And then suddenly he died of a heart attack. This was a shock to her as in the back of her mind was the thought, the hope, that some day he would return to stay.

His death made a lot of things seem meaningless, among them the frame of reference her New England grandmother had given her. She had graduated from college by this time, and she decided that she wanted to look around for a bit before deciding what she wanted to do. She travelled, worked at temporary jobs when she needed money. For a while she lived in a commune but was soon disillusioned, as the members seemed more interested in rituals like eating vegetarian food or keeping their children naked rather than making any constructive effort towards a communal life. She grew tired of their self-absorption and irresponsible drifting life and went back to college. Then her grandmother died and this gave her the final push towards the decision to go to India.

If she had not gone to India she would not have met Gurunath. She met him at the Kirtikars' on the day of Sujata's birthday party. He came late and Sujata was full of an intense happiness (everything about Sujata was intense) when she saw him.

He said to Susan, "You are an American, aren't you?"

"Does it show?"

"Which category of Americans do you belong to?"

She thought, Oh God, one of those American-hater types.

"Are there categories?" she said.

"Well, there is the escapist and adventurer. Then there is the academician who wants to come to India so he chooses to study something which will enable him to do so at someone's cost. Then there is the tourist intent on imbibing the five-star culture. And the lowest category is the Christian missionary who actually manages to convince himself that he has come here to do good."

He was probably the best-looking man Susan had seen. With his wheat colouring, brilliant green eyes and brown hair, he was almost beautiful. For this reason she mistrusted him.

She said with deliberate coolness, "Let me see. I think I belong a little to each of your categories. There is a bit of an adventurer in everyone. Then I am here on the excuse of studying Hinduism and Buddhism because I could not afford the trip without a scholarship. I haven't been here long enough to be fed up with the squalor and filth, but I expect I will in due course. And last, I am not a missionary, but I am the next best thing, the daughter of one."

She was poised for a fight but his next remark threw her off balance. "I owe you an apology," he said with a charming smile. "I had no idea. I didn't mean to insult your father."

She could not resist the retort. "You mean you intended to insult missionaries generally, but not my father particularly."

"If you insist on putting it that way. Were does you father work?"

"Did. He is dead."

"I am sorry. Where did he work?"

"A place called Savli."

"Have you been there?"

"No, but I mean to, just as soon as I am settled."

"What did he do?"

"He was a medical missionary."

"He must have worked at the Savli hospital then."

"He was one of the founders of the hospital."

"I see. Where did you meet Sujata?"

"Right here."

"You mean she just pulled your name out of the hat and invited you to her party?"

"I live here."

"I really have been out of touch. Will you kindly explain yourself?"

She laughed. It was difficult not to. "There's nothing to explain. The Kirtikars are members of the Indo-American Friendship Club. Their name is on a list of families who would like to have American students stay with them. I was assigned to them."

He wandered off to join a group around Sujata, but towards the end of the evening he was at her side again.

"Susan, how about letting me drive you to Savli this Sunday?"

"You don't have to bother. It's only about sixty miles. It can't take more than an hour by bus."

"How fast do you think buses travel here? Sixty miles will take at least three hours."

"So let it."

"I would like to take you, unless you'd rather go alone."

"I'd be happy to go with you."

"It's settled then. I'll pick you up around eight." He turned to Sujata who had joined them. "Are you coming, Sujata? Susan and I are going to Savli to see the hospital where her father worked."

"No, I don't think so."

"Come on, what else have you got to do on a Sunday?"

His question spoiled any chance there might have been of persuading Sujata to change her mind. She said, "Do you think only you have important things to do?"

"No, of course not. You have lots of important things to do, especially on Sunday. Right?"

"Right."

Susan wondered if the brother-sister kind of bickering hid something else. She was just as glad that Sujata was not going with them.

Later that evening Sujata asked her how she liked Guru. Susan said she hadn't known him long enough to decide.

"That means you don't like him."

"Not necessarily. He is very good-looking, I'll grant you that. Is there a reason why I should decide to like him?"

"What do you mean?"

"You, Sujata."

"Oh no," Sujata laughed. "There's nothing like that." Then she added, "Nobody owns Guru."

"He sounds like a member of the lost species of untamed men. Where did you get to know him?"

"Guru's father lived with us in the same block of flats in Bombay until Papa retired and we came to live here. Of course Guru was not there much of the time. He went to school and college in America. But he came to spend some of the holidays with his father. And then I got to really know him when he finished his education and came to live with his father."

"How did he happen to be educated in America?"

"His mother is an American, you know."

"That explains his American accent. He talked of my Americanness showing."

It explained something else as well, she thought. His initial antagonism to her and the defensive attitude about India. The mark of a fresh convert? And then, in spite of everything, the way they had got along easily.

"Why did he come back to live here?"

"I suppose he decided that his father deserved him for a few years. Thakurkaka was a very lonely man. He drove himself very hard and kept himself very busy so that people wouldn't realize it. But Guru saw it. He was so happy when Guru decided to stay here. It almost made up for all the years of loneliness. And it was good for Guru also. After all, a son needs a father, don't you think?"

Susan thought that much of what Sujata said, and the way she said it, sounded as though it had been picked up from her mother. Maybe also the final hackneyed sentiment.

She said, "I wouldn't know."

Savli turned out to be quite a big town, much larger than the small village Susan had expected from her father's descriptions. The hospital, a big ugly gray building surrounded by several smaller structures of various sizes and styles, was at one end of the town. They met a young medical officer on duty, who referred them to Dr. Rao. As Dr. Rao did not attend hospital on Sunday, they went to his house. He was delighted to meet Susan. He said that he and Dr. Wilkes had been very close friends, and insisted that Susan and Gurunath stay for lunch. A gaunt, grizzled man, he spoke of Susan's father in very formal terms.

"Most doctors become quickly anesthetized to pain and sickness and poverty, especially if they work in a place like this. But your father was one of the rare men who retained their compassion for the poor and the sick. His patients worshipped him. He had a marvellous knack for dealing with people. It was not just a skill he had developed, it came from an inner liking for people."

They had spent many of their off-duty hours together, Dr. Rao said, "and Dr. Wilkes often ended the evening by taking his dinner with us." Yet, there was nothing in Dr. Rao's conversation to indicate that the two men had been anything more than colleagues. There was no reference to Dr. Wilkes's personal life, no affectionate narration of a foible. Dr. Rao spoke with the distance of reverence, and Susan wondered if it was for her benefit.

She and Guru looked around the hospital and then visited the house where her father had lived. It was now occupied by Dr. Kanhere who was most cordial and insisted on giving them a conducted tour of the house and tea afterwards. Susan realized that the house must have looked quite different when her father had lived in it. Dr. Kanhere had three small children and he kept apologizing for the untidiness of the house. Nevertheless, Susan felt that she was suddenly in the presence of something which had been a tangible part of her father's life. This was the house which he left every morning when he went to work and returned to every evening, to relax, to eat the meal cooked by his housekeeper, perhaps to read and write, perhaps to feel lonely, to miss her. No, that was just wishful thinking.

During the ride back she was depressed and silent. Gurunath said, "Sentimental pilgrimages are not always a good idea, you know."

"I always asked him a lot of questions about the hospital, his house, the town. It's difficult to think about a person in a vacuum, and I wanted to visualize the place. But what he wrote about it never brought it alive to me. Now I know why. There is nothing to bring alive in the place. Nothing beautiful. It's just a shabby little town, dirty, dusty, scrubby. What made him want to spend his life here?"

"Maybe he didn't care about his surroundings. His work was all that mattered to him."

"The complete professional."

She was crying.

"Susan!"

"There was no room in his life for anything personal. I bet he was happy when my mother died, so he could bundle me off to Grandma and forget about me. Then nothing need interfere with his work."

"Come now, that's not fair."

"Why not? Who was the gentle loving man with a real feeling for people, who could make his patients worship him? I never knew him. The man I knew didn't even know how to talk to me. What happened to his knack of dealing with people when he was with me? Or did he give so much of himself to these poor miserable people that he had nothing left over to give me?"

"Here." He passed a large white handkerchief to her.

"I am sorry. I had no right to subject you to that temper tantrum."

"Feel better now?"

She smiled. "Much better."

"It's not much use blaming other people, especially your parents, even when you feel they deserve blame. They did the best they could, and you have to pick up and go on from there."

"That's a fine philosophy, if you can follow it."

As they neared Poona he said, "Why don't we have dinner before I leave you home?"

"I would love that, but I probably look a mess. Besides, I have told them I would be home for dinner."

"That's easily put right. We'll go to my apartment where you can have a wash and call home."

When they reached his place he said, "Tell you what. Why don't we see if Sujata will join us?"

Susan felt as though she had hurtled down from a pinnacle. She said, "That's a wonderful idea."

It turned out that Sujata had gone to the movies. Susan had been looking around the apartment. She said, "This is a surprise. I expected an untidy place, an unmade bed, a litter of books and clothes everywhere, dirty coffee cups. And instead, this."

He laughed. "It's a fallacious feminine theory that a man can't live in clean, well-cared-for surroundings without the help of a woman."

"You can't tell me you do all this yourself."

"Of course not. I have a man who manages everything very unobtrusively."

She wandered into the bedroom. There were slippers by the bed, books on the bedside table — ranging from Ian Fleming to Bertrand Russell — two newspapers neatly folded, a magazine rack, a shoe-rack. No trivial accumulations, no traces of permanent occupancy. It looked more like a hotel suite than someone's home.

She said, "It's a frightening place. It hears no imprint of any human being. Everything is in such perfect order that I would be afraid to touch anything. It would be almost like violating a law of nature to wrinkle that bedspread."

He lit a cigarette and sat down on the bed.

"Your conclusions are only academic. I quite often have people in here who not only wrinkle the bedspread but track mud into the living room and spill a drink on the carpet."

"And after they are gone, your man simply wipes out all traces of their presence. Unobtrusively, of course."

"And without looking at me accusingly or moaning about a stain on his precious carpet. Would you like a drink?"

"That you, yes. Especially if I am allowed to spill it."

"You are perfectly free to spill it."

He took her to the Four Seasons which he said served the best food in town.

"I eat here frequently when I am in Poona."

"You don't live here all the time?"

"I spend half my time in Bombay."

"And you eat out the whole time you are here?"

"And the whole time I am in Bombay."

"Why?"

"I am against establishing a household."

"Isn't it dreary eating in a restaurant all the time?"

"On the contrary, I can have much better food here than in any home I know. Also a much wider variety."

"You may have a point," she said doubtfully.

His sudden loud laugh was startling. "You don't really want to believe it. No woman does. It's a personal affront to her that a man can manage very well without a woman to keep house and cook for him."

A little later he asked her, "Why did you come here, Susan? You were disappointed today. What had you expected to find?" The unexpected gentleness of his voice almost brought on tears.

"I don't know."

"You must have had some idea what you wanted out of this trip."

"I hadn't thought very clearly. I guess basically I was just curious to see the place where he lived. I thought I could recapture something of what he had been, from visiting the place. But of course dead men don't leave traces, unless they want to. I thought maybe I would find something, some sign, that he cared about me. But there was nothing, because there was no place in his life for me. He denied my existence."

"Susan, does it occur to you that you are reading too much purpose in his actions? The element of choice involved may not have been as clear cut as you think. He came here as a young man, he had already worked here a number of years before he was suddenly faced with a choice. By that time he may have come to think of this as his life's work. It's difficult to make a fresh start elsewhere. So he just stayed on."

"What you mean is that he was just a third-rate doctor who had found his niche and was afraid of leaving it. Don't look so shocked. I've had it said to me. People like him come here because there's no competition, not in the kind of work they do. They are appreciated even if they are not very good. And they are smart enough to realize that they wouldn't stand a chance of making a mark in their own country. But all this still doesn't explain why he couldn't have kept me here with him."

They concentrated on eating for a while, then she said, "Why did you decide to settle here?"

He looked surprised and she realized that she had admitted that she had discussed him behind his back. She said, "I asked Sujata how come you had an American accent and she told me you did most of your growing-up there. So what made you come back here?"

"Maybe I was smart too, like your father."

"That's not a good enough reason, in your case."

"Well, I was here for a visit. Dad asked me what I intended to do. I had nothing specific in mind, so I decided to stay here for a while and work with him."

"What did he do?"

"He edited a small newspaper."

"What did you study?"

"All sorts of things. Actually I've had the most haphazard education because I couldn't make up my mind what I wanted to do. I studied French, journalism, anatomy, history of art. For a while I thought I would became a doctor. Then I thought I would paint. But I didn't stick to anything for very long."

"What do you do now?"

"Nothing on a regular basis. I do articles and illustrations for newspapers and magazines as a freelancer. Once in a while I paint. I travel."

"I would like to see your paintings."

"They are not worth seeing. You can take my word for it. I am not very good, but I don't care. I enjoy life too much to beat my brains out trying to do something I know I can't."

When he left her home he stopped to say hello to Sujata.

"How was your movie?"

"Very good."

"I suppose you needed the relaxation after doing all those important things all day."

"Of course. I hope your day was not too strenuous."

"On the contrary, it was highly enjoyable."

After this Guru took Susan out a lot, sightseeing or to the movies or to dinner. Sujata was not included in the invitations. Mrs. Kirtikar remarked that it was very kind of Guru to take her out and Sujata said one day, "I hope you are not taking Guru seriously."

"What do you mean?"

"I mean I hope you are not falling in love with him or anything."

"It so happens I am not, but is there a particular reason why I shouldn't?"

"He doesn't want permanent involvements. Especially not with an American girl."

"Why not?"

"He doesn't want to be his father all over again. His parents married while his father was studying in America. His mother didn't want to come here at all, but finally did when her husband wouldn't agree to live there. But she didn't even try to make a go of it here. When Guru was about five she left with him on the excuse that he must be educated there. After that she spent most of her time there, and kept Guru with her. She wasn't even here when Guru's father died."

"She could hardly help that."

"They had wired her when he was seriously ill and in hospital."

"We won't argue about that because I don't know enough about the circumstances. But even granting that his mother was a fickle and irresponsible woman, Guru can't be childish enough to think that all American women are like that."

"Well, it's true that Americans don't respect the institution of marriage."

"What nonsense! We respect it as much as you do. We simply don't believe in dragging on a marriage that's become untenable. That's more honest."

"I thought you were not serious about him."

"I am not. I am merely arguing a point."

About this time Gurunath left Poona and Susan told herself that this was good because she needed time to think things out. Also, an idea about a book on her father's life was taking shape in her mind, and she wanted to go back to Savli to discuss it with Dr. Rao, and ask him if he would help her with it. He said of course, but she would have to stay in Savli for a few days, as commuting would be troublesome, and he had spare time only at night. So why didn't she go and stay with them? His wife would be happy to have her.

Susan went to Savli and talked to Dr. Rao and the other doctors who had worked with her father. She interviewed some of his patients, read through his case histories. Dr. Rao said that her father's most important work had been in the feild of tuberculosis, and he had intended, with the help of the case histories, to write a book about his findings.

The most significant outcome of her trip was that she saw that she would have to come to terms with whatever her father was. Just as there was no point in blaming him, there was none in tearing him down to flay herself. He had done good work here, and he was remembered with respect and affection by countless people. He had helped people not only by diagnosing their ills and prescribing treatment but often also by paying out of his own pocket for their medicines, food, travel. These were facts and she would simply accept them, not wonder why a man who gave so much to others withheld himself so completely from her.

She felt at peace with herself. Life at Savli gave her a sense of serenity. When she thought of Guru at all, it was with a detachment on which she congratulated herself. He was just a passing phase. She didn't even know him very well. And in any case she didn't want to get involved with him if he had all sorts of complexes about American women just because he felt his mother had let his father down. She forgot to what extent he had got under her skin until she returned to Poona and felt a sharp disappointment that he was not back yet. And then a sudden lift of pleasure when she finally saw him again.

He had tickets for an Arthur Miller play being produced by an amateur theatre group on Sunday afternoon, and invited Susan and Sujata to go with him. Sujata haughtily declined the invitation, saying she had another engagement. Susan asked him on Sunday, "Was Sujata mad at you because you invited me to the play?"

"Why should she be?"

"If she has a special claim on you, she would."

"Nobody has a special claim on me. Besides, she is too young."

Susan wanted to ask too young for what, but she only said, "She's awfully attractive."

"That she is."

Susan had almost hoped that he would say he didn't go for that type.

The play, *Death of a Salesman*, turned out to be not very good. When they returned, Sujata crowed over them. "I knew it wasn't going to be good. That's why I didn't come."

"I thought you had another engagement."

"That too, of course."

"Who was the lucky guy?"

159

Sujata refused to answer but her mother supplied the information that the lucky guy was an undesirable character with a cinema-actorish get-up called Mahesh Khanna.

Susan continued seeing Guru and, notwithstanding Sujata's warning, derived hope from the mere fact that he chose to spend so much time with her. There developed between them an easy friendliness which sometimes disturbed her by its very absence of conflict.

Guru had considered Mahesh a bit of a joke, but Sujata was seeing too much of him. Her mother was alarmed, but Sujata simply laughed at her protests. Sujata's father, who was having one of his periodic attacks of asthma, could not be bothered. Finally, Mrs. Kirtikar pleaded with Guru to talk to Sujata. He said it would be useless, but she told him to try anyway. So he tried. He said that Mahesh was a year junior to her in college after having failed twice, whereas she was a brilliant student. He had been seen with half-a-dozen different girls in the past few months. He was known to be associated with the *gunda* element in the college. In short, he was simply not worthy of her. Sujata told him coldly that whom she picked for friends was entirely her own business, and she was not accountable to him. Besides, she refused to discuss Mahesh with him anyway, because he had not even taken the trouble to meet Mahesh before making false allegations about him on the strength of malicious gossip.

After this Sujata understandably turned down Guru's invitation to a picnic at Mahabaleshwar. He wanted to show Susan, he said, that all of India was not scrubby and ugly. Sujata said he was welcome to do so without the benefit of her company. Susan asked him if he was disappointed that Sujata was not coming and he said no, he had no patience with temperamental adolescents.

It was just after the monsoon and Mahabaleshwar was glorious with the washed green of the trees and the bright red of the earth and the clear view of the valleys and the ranges of

mountains beyond. Susan was enchanted. They walked miles
of unfrequented trails and ate a picnic lunch and lay down
under the trees to rest. The ground was uneven and there were
insects crawling about, but she didn't mind any of it as she
watched the sunlight filtering through the trees above them
and talked about her studies and the book about her father
and finally fell silent. She turned her head towards him and
he kissed her and said, "There are panthers in this jungle, you
know."

She said, "I don't care if one comes and kills me. I would
like to freeze this moment and keep it forever and the only way
to do it would be to die right now." But she was very happy
and death was far from her thoughts.

She said, as though it was just an idle question, "What do
you see in me, Guru? A man like you can have his pick of
girls who are more beautiful, more attractive, cleverer than I
am."

He sat up, looked at her a moment and said, "You are
plump and pretty and fun to be with. You know how to enjoy
life without worrying about tomorrow. Besides, being an
American, you are sensible enough to know that dating a man
a few times and being kissed by him is not being practically
married to him."

Her throat went dry. She felt cold. She closed her eyes so that
he wouldn't see the sudden hurt in them.

"Was that all it was, the past few months?"

He looked at her with surprise and said, "Of course. Don't
tell me you thought it was anything more. After all, I can't be
the first man you have dated."

"The first who has meant anything to me."

"And so you have convinced yourself that you are in love
with me. Listen, Susie, don't make the mistake that too many
girls make, by thinking that having a good time with someone
is the same as falling in love with him."

"Don't you love me at all?"

161

"Sure, I love you. I am very fond of you, so I'll tell you something, though I don't think I owe you an explanation. Even if I think of falling in love with a girl and marrying, I can never marry you."

"Why?"

"It simply wouldn't work. The cards would be pretty well stacked against us."

"You are trying to punish your mother through me."

He smiled. "Everything doesn't have a simple explanation, Susie. This has nothing to do with my mother. Come now, dry your eyes and stop being a fool. Some day you will thank me for having the good sense not to involve us both in an impossible relationship."

For a while, after Susan returned home, things seemed to go well for her. She got her Ph. D. and a teaching job in a small college. The book about her father finally took shape as a novel based on his life, and was well received. All this helped heal some of the laceration her ego had received at Guru's hands. She sent a copy of her book to Guru, feeling that she had somehow accomplished a partial revenge, and was deflated when she received no response from him, not even an acknowledgment.

Then she received the wedding invitation. She thought, it seems that Sujata is no longer young. She also thought, with considerable bitterness, that is the Indian way. One girl to have fun with, another to marry. That was the lesson Guru had meant her to learn. He was not going to make his father's mistake. Only a stupid and impractical man marries the girl he loves without stopping to think of the future.

Slowly she began to get bored with her job. Instead of being comfortingly small, the college where she taught now seemed narrow and suffocatingly provincial. The students, instead of being bright and responsive kids as she had thought at first, were wide-eyed and shallow. A second novel she had started was going badly, and she knew that her colleagues, though solicitous on the surface, were relieved that they were not going to have a celebrity living among them. She hated the thought that her creativity had dried up after having written the one book that everybody is supposed to have in them.

Perhaps if she had married, she would have sunk happily into domesticity and none of this would have mattered. But she did not meet anyone even remotely eligible.

Several times she considered suicide. She would leave a letter which would reach Guru after her death.

And then suddenly, when she had almost given in to the pall of depression, she heard Guru and Sujata were divorced. She took this as a sign and decided to return to India.

She was surprised at the ease with which Guru slipped back into her life. After all her wondering and agonizing, he accepted her quite matter-of-factly.

She asked him what had happened to his marriage and he said, "Same thing that happens to all marriages which end in a divorce. It didn't work."

"You'd rather not talk about it?"

"There's nothing to talk about. We didn't get along, that's all."

Susan rented a room which for an extra payment the landlord furnished with an iron cot, a table and chair and a small cupboard. She bought a stove and a few pots and pans.

Near the top of her list of priorities was losing weight. Looking at herself through Guru's eyes, she saw herself as not just a little too plump but disgustingly fat, an exaggerated cartoon character.

She discovered that there were other changes in Guru, not just his looks. He now did a bi-weekly column of social and political comment for a well-known newspaper. She read clippings of some of his articles and was impressed. They were very readable, and she realized that the amount of work and organization which a regular column must involve indicated that he was taking himself much more seriously than he ever had.

She eased herself into the habit of doing a lot of the spade work for him, reading several papers and filing clippings. At first she offered help timidly and derived great pleasure from being allowed to do something for him. Then imperceptibly the pleasure turned to resentment when he accepted her efforts without a word of appreciation. She felt exploited. This was one of the changes in him that alarmed her.

She also found that the old easy friendliness between them was absent. He was not as even-tempered as he used to be. He was often tired and irritable or morose and uncommunicative. She found it a strain to adapt herself to his changing moods. When he was in town she found herself jittery and tense, forever trying to please and fearing that she didn't. And when he was away she found herself unable to think of anything except him, weaving impossible daydreams around him.

She tried to settle down to her own writing but was far from pleased with what she did and succeeded, day after day, only in filling a waste-basket. She kept going simply by abstaining from thinking about anything but the next few days.

The only thing to be pleased about was that she did not find it hard to stick to an almost starvation diet. She lost weight steadily. When she lost her twentieth pound she planned a celebration. She cooked a festive meal and Guru brought wine. She had gone to the expense of getting a new dress made, a wine-red raw cotton which she knew suited her dark hair and brown eyes. She knew she looked attractive, and she was in high spirits. Guru's eyes were bright with a smile and he seemed relaxed. It was almost like old times. She was light-headed with the wine, otherwise she would not have talked about his marriage.

"Tell me, Guru, how did you ever get roped into marriage in the first place?"

"The usual reasons," he said shortly.

Having started treading dangerous ground, she was reckless. "What are the usual reasons for a man like you? I can think of one. Marriage might be the only way to get the woman you want. Was that it?"

He said nothing and she quickly said, "I am sorry. I shouldn't have said that."

Nothing indicated whether he had accepted her apology or not.

"Guru, you profess not to believe in marriage, yet you gave her a chance. Why won't you give me a chance? I admit I am not nearly as good-looking as she is, but we have much more in common than you and she ever had. We can make a great team."

He said, his voice under very tight control, "If it was wrong for us then, Susie, it's wrong for us now. Nothing has happened to change things."

The calm certainty of his voice frightened her. Too late, she knew that she had overstepped the limit that he had implicitly laid down for her. She tried to pretend that it was a game and said with a sigh, "Oh well, if I remain a spinster I can at least tell myself it was not for lack of trying."

She gave a high-pitched giggle which sounded horrible, and on that note the evening, which had promised so much, ended.

She could not accept the conclusion that she was totally unattractive to him, or that he liked his freedom too well to marry. There must be another woman. And so when he returned from his next trip to Bombay she asked him, "Who is the girlfriend?'

If she were off the mark, he would merely look perplexed and say he didn't know what she was talking about. But he said quietly, "It's none of your business."

"Oh I know it's none of my business. I am only a charity case after all. Why should you be accountable to me?"

165

He said, still in that menacingly quiet voice, "You are damned right I am not accountable to you. You had better remember it the next time you feel like saying something stupid."

She had only succeeded in finding out that he was capable of cruelty. What was she doing to herself and him? Was it like this between him and Sujata? Suddenly she felt she had to see Sujata, talk to her. She had avoided the Kirtikars because she did not want to see Sujata. Now they were so happy to see her that she felt guilty about not having gone to see them earlier.

It was not difficult to manoeuvre the conversation around to Sujata's marriage and divorce.

Her mother said, "They are both too independent and strong-willed. I wasn't in favour of the marriage, but you know Sujata. She doesn't listen to anyone's advice."

"Did she take the divorce very hard?"

"She didn't seem to, but then Sujata is not the sort who cries on anyone's shoulder. Actually I think Guru took it harder than she did. I suppose at his age he thinks it difficult to make a fresh start. She is younger and more resilient. One of these days I hope she gets married. It's not nice for a young woman to live alone in a big city."

"Doesn't she live here with you?"

"No, she lives in Bombay, didn't you know? You know she was always interested in dressmaking. Now she does it commercially. She runs a boutique. She says Poona is too small a town to give scope for her talent."

Something was exploding in Susan's head. Mrs. Kirtikar was asking her how long she planned to stay this time and why she didn't come and stay with them, and offering her a plate of sweets. Somehow she managed to make the proper responses and made her escape after promising to look in again soon. She took a rickshaw to Guru's place, hoping to catch him before he left for dinner. He opened the door himself.

"Why are you sitting in the dark, Guru?"

She started switching on a light and he said, "Don't. It's more peaceful in the dark." He had a drink in his hand and offered her one.

"Thank you, I don't think I want one now. I want to talk to you."

"Sorry I can't offer to take you out to dinner, because I am not eating today. I am not feeling very well."

"I just want to talk to you."

"Can't it wait? As I said, I am not feeling very well."

He did look tired and drawn and the lines on his face seemed deeper than usual. He had the sort of face that wouldn't age gracefully. She wanted to tell him that she loved him and that if he loved her, nothing else would matter.

She said instead, "No, it can't wait."

She walked to his desk and sat down on its edge. ·

"It's Sujata you are seeing in Bombay, isn't it? It's always been Sujata. I was such a fool I actually believed what you said. I really thought that the rules which govern ordinary men didn't apply to you. Poor Guru." She began to laugh.

"Stop it, Susie."

She wondered how far he would go if he got really angry. Would he hit her? She wished he would. That would prove that they were equals.

"Sujata and you. It's no good, Guru. It never was."

"It's none of your business."

"You've made it my business by using me as a pawn in your game all along. And I was too dense to catch on to it."

"Have you finished?"

"Yes."

"Then get out."

She slid off the table and went to him.

"It doesn't have to be like this, you know." She put her hand tentatively on his arm but he shook it off roughly.

167

She said, "I am glad someone can put you through the same hell you put me through."

She walked out of the apartment slowly, ready to turn back if he called her. In all these years her capacity to dream had remained unimpaired.

She walked back to her room through the still crowded streets, hands dug deep into her pockets, and action symbolic, she thought, of her wish not to have anything to do with the people. The chaotic quality of the streets in the evening had always made her nervous. She felt no affinity with these people. She thought of her father with anger because long ago he had sent her away, so that what she thought of with nostalgia now was not the dusty miserable village where he had lived but the lovely tree-lined street where she grew up, the scent of a pine forest, the smoke rising from a charcoal-broiled steak.

She thought, Guru said I shouldn't blame my father. By the same logic I shouldn't blame Guru. I gave him the chance to use me because I wanted to use him, the same way I wanted to use my father, as a crutch.

It's time I stood on my own feet. Guru never loved me, so I've lost nothing. Why did I want to settle for a lukewarm one-sided relationship? The hell with him. But that's not strictly true. I might start by being honest with myself. If he crooks his finger even now, I'd want to go back to him on his terms, crawl back and take anything he offered me. But I'm not going to, and that is strictly true. All that is finished, done with.

Susan Wilkes alone against the world. It's an unequal fight, but I've got to carry it on because something in me won't let go. That's what I have finally learned. To endure, perhaps to prevail — that is the only triumph.

She let herself into her room and switched on the light. She took the plastic cover off her portable Olivetti and rolled in a fresh sheet of paper, conscious of going through the steps of an important ritual. She felt a surge of power as her fingers flew over the keys with demented speed.

It was the end and the beginning.

# THE TORTURER

For the first time in weeks I can draw in a breath without scorching my nostrils. The thunderstorm has spent itself as swiftly as it had gathered. Everything looks cool and green but limp from the violence of the lashing rain. In a corner of the garden I see a stooping figure working with the fierce concentration that only children and senile people bestow on trifles.

"What are you doing out there in the damp, Father?" I call out.

"Pulling out weeds," he answers. "This is the time to get at them, when the soil is wet and soft."

I do not question the soundness of his ideas about gardening. It is only a pitiful attempt on his part to prove his usefulness. For he is old and useless and failing rapidly. It was a difficult job getting him to leave Nimbgao. He agreed to come only after I had convinced him that I needed him here. Otherwise every time he fell ill I would receive a telegram from a neighbour. It was inconvenient and awkward to ask for leave each time. He still maintains that he is only here on a short visit. But he knows, and I know that the visit is to last until the end comes for him.

This is the man whom I hated and feared, and then pitied with a pity one feels for a starving stray dog, dirty and uncared for because he has no one to turn to. But now nothing — not even pity — binds me to him. I am free. Here in the midst of my family I think of the past as belonging to another world, another life. I sometimes wonder if he thinks of the past as I do. Or is he still an integral part of it?

When I think of Nimbgao, I think of the enormous kitchen in our rambling ancestral house. Most of my childhood memories are connected with the kitchen because it was there

170

that I spent evening after evening with my head in my mother's lap, fighting off sleep. She never made me go to bed, as she never forced me to do anything. So I kept her company while she waited for Father. He came home late, sometimes as late as midnight. If Mother questioned him about where he had been, he just laughed.

I always remember Mother like this, her face glowing faintly in the light of the woodfire which burned low to keep the food warm. She represented everything that was good and beautiful and wronged. To my child's way of thinking the world was as simple as that. The clash between good and bad, the bad distilled in the person of my father. I was not aware then that there is a kind of goodness which brings out the badness in others.

That was what helped keep me awake, this nightly nursing of my hate. Love can envelop you in its warmth and release you into a deep, dreamless sleep. But never hate. I should know. It was hate which churned in me, gnawed at my insides, till I was unable to rest, but could sleep only fitfully when I was tired beyond endurance.

"What are you just sitting in the corner for?" Father invariably bellowed in a jovial way on his return. "Don't you have anything to do?"

"I am tired," Mother would say in her weak voice that was barely above a whisper.

"What have you got to be tired about? It's not as if you did any work."

Silence from Mother. This goaded him into ranting some more. His favourite theme was how he could never see a cheerful face around the house. At this point he would act as if he had just seen me. He would give me a heartily slap on the back which made me wince with terror.

"What are you doing up so late, boy?" He never called me by my name, as far back as I can remember.

"Keeping Mother company," I would mutter sullenly.

171

Then he would whirl on her. "Don't you know any better than to keep the child awake so late?"

He then packed me off to bed, where I strained my ears towards the kitchen until I drifted into troubled sleep.

As far as I know, Father never had to work for a living, and he preferred to loaf rather than do a day's honest work. He knew a little about Ayurvedic medicine, and now and again people came to him for advice. He did not take money for treating them, because the feeling of importance it gave him was more important to him than money. My grandfather was a lawyer who practised at the taluka court. By a whim which brought him the ridicule of the whole town, he put his life's savings into buying the Ghost Palaces. These were three large dilapidated mansions outside town which used to be the haunt of a notorious bandit. He had been dead and gone for years, but the houses had been lying vacant. It was believed that the bandit's ghost haunted them to guard the treasure that he had buried somewhere within them. Anyway, Grandfather said it was his money to burn and bought the property for a song. Then he put in some more money repairing and remodelling the houses into rentable flats.

Either the old man was shrewder than anybody gave him credit for, or he was just lucky. An ordnance factory was built near by during the First World War. That brought a lot of new people to the vicinity. The demand for housing grew overnight. With the influx of newcomers, the ghost legend died down and Grandfather triumphantly rented his apartments. Father has always lived on this income. Of course the rent remained stationary while the cost of living went on going up, but Father has always got enough out of the investment to keep up our old house after a fashion and live fairly comfortably. I say after a fashion because there have never been any repairs made to the house in my memory. No modern amenities were ever installed. Mother had to cook on a woodfire and get red and swollen eyes from the smoke when the neighbours had begun to use coal, and later kerosene. Father never got pipes put for water so that Mother had to carry all the water we needed from the old well in the back of the house. She was delicate and frail, and I never knew how she coped with the work. When I grew up I used to help her as much as I could. But I had to be very cautious about it, because if Father caught me at it he gave me a thrashing and chased me away, shouting, "Is that all you were born for, to do a woman's work? Why can't you go out and play, like other children?"

My memories are all disjointed, and there is no chronological order to them. I remember, for instance, the day I was sent to school. One morning Father suddenly said, "Come on, boy, I'm taking you to school."

I was eight years old then. "I don't want to go to school," I said. "I want to stay home with Mother."

At that he laughed until the tears came to his eyes. Then he scowled and said, "Stay home with Mother indeed. Come on before I whip you."

At the threat of physical harm my bravery evaporated. I gave Mother an appealing glance. If she had given the word, I would have gone happily. But she refused to say anything. She just stood in the kitchen door, her eyes streaming with tears.

"What's there to cry about? Anybody would think I was taking him to his own funeral instead of to school."

Mother put her hands on her ears with a pained expression and I meekly followed Father to school.

I hated him for this, for I was certain that he did it only to keep me away from Mother. I was miserable in school at first, but soon learned to like it. Studies offered something objective on which I could concentrate, and school kept me away from the tension-charged atmosphere at home for a few hours.

There is another incident vividly etched in my memory. Since starting school I had learned to go to bed early. One night something awakened me. It could have been the draught created by the front door opening, or some faint sound. I got out of bed and crept towards the kitchen. Mother was as usual sitting by the fire, her knees drawn up and her head on her folded arms. Father went and knelt by her and pulled her violently into his arms. She must have been asleep, for she awoke with a startled scream. When she realized what was happening, she pushed Father away and cried, "Don't touch me."

He stood up unsteadily and said, "I'm you husband. Don't you remember me?" in a kind of singsong sardonic voice.

She looked at him with distaste and whispered, "You're drunk."

"That's right. You have hit it on the head. I wouldn't have tried anything so foolish if I had been sober."

His voice was full of bitterness. Then he turned and saw me.

"Am I never to be free of this brat?" he cried.

He looked so ominous that I was sure that he was going to beat me. I ran to Mother.

"He's your own son, how can your tongue utter such words about him?" Mother held me close to her, as if for protection. She was trembling.

"I'm beginning to have doubts about that," Father flung at her and walked out. It was only when the door closed behind him that I felt easy.

Mother began to sob.

"Don't be afraid," I said. "I shall always take care of you."

"He didn't even eat," she said incongruously.

"Let him go without his meal. Let him starve to death." She quickly put her hand on my mouth.

"You shouldn't talk like that," she said. "You must never talk like that."

I was a coward and Father took a peculiar pleasure in torturing Mother in front of me. He loved to watch the impotent rage struggle inside me and never dare to find expression.

"You call yourself a woman," he said once. "But you don't know the first thing about being a woman. You should take some lessons from Shanti." Shanti was one of the town's prostitutes.

Mother gasped, shocked out of her habitual calm. "How can you utter the name of that immoral woman in my presence?"

"Why not? As I said, there are a lot of things she can teach you. You can't even perform the one task you were created for — to bear children. Look at that thing you gave birth to."

I shrank back as if to avoid a blow.

"Look at that sickly thing. Do you call it a boy? Always lurking in shadows, always afraid of things, hiding behind your sari."

"You can say anything you want to me, but leave the boy alone."

"Why?" he asked with excessive politeness. "Let him ask me to leave him alone, then I'll think about it. Isn't he old enough to speak for himself? What do you say, boy?"

"Nothing, Father,"

"Nothing, Father," he mimicked me. Then he suddenly shouted. "Get out of here, both of you. I'm sick of the sight of you." He covered his face with his hands, and his body shook, but whether from sobbing or laughing I couldn't tell.

That was how it went on, this cat-and-mouse way, until I was sixteen. Mother fell ill. I don't know what was wrong with her. She didn't have a doctor. She just looked pale and sick and went about her work more silently and sadly than usual. Then one morning I woke up and found the kitchen empty, the fire unlit. I found Mother in bed, and when I touched her forehead it felt burning hot. For minutes I stood confused. Such an emergency had never arisen before. Thin and frail though she was, Mother had never known illness. Finally I decided that I must go and get a doctor. But I was too late. Father was already up and I met him in the hall.

"What's all this? Why isn't my tea ready?" he shouted.

"I think Mother is sick," I said, trying to control the trembling which seized me at the prospect of confrontation with him. He saw that I had my chappals on.

"And where do you think you are going?"

"To get a doctor."

"Doctor! There's nothing wrong with your mother. I'm doctor enough to know that. Come on, get yourself up. Let's see some activity around this dead place." This last was addressed to her. A moment later she appeared in the hall, her hair dishevelled, her eyes dilated with fever and a strange kind of light which I couldn't define and which frightened me. She weaved her way to the kitchen and I started to follow her.

"Where do you think you are going? Don't you have school today?"

"I am not going to school."

"Why?" he asked in a soft menacing voice.

"Mother is not well. Somebody ought to help her with the work."

"Who said you could be that somebody?"

My heart was beginning to pound sickeningly, and I felt a hot flush spreading from by ears up to my temples.

"Who else is there?" I said.

"The devil. Don't you know, boy? Your mother has a pact with the devil." Then he suddenly bellowed, "Go on. Go this minute or I promise I'll break both your legs. Then you can sit here with your mother all the rest of your life."

Five minutes later I was headed towards school.


I could see the crowd from a long way away as I walked home that afternoon. Nobody ever visited us, so it could mean only one thing. I had a strange calm feeling as if I had expected it to happen. I learned later that Mother had lost her balance while drawing water out of the well. At the moment I didn't care about the details. I knew only that she was dead, and I felt a quiet determined rage. He had killed her and I was going to kill him.

I walked past the people into the house. Father was standing in the middle of the kitchen. At the sight of him my rage boiled. I ran at him.

"You — you killed her. You killed my mother," I screamed at him in my squeaky adolescent voice. I had lost my fear of him. I was shouting and choking on my tears all at the same time.

He looked blankly at me, as though he wasn't really taking in what I was saying. Now that my eyes were used to the comparative darkness of the kitchen I could see his face.

He wore the lost bewildered expression of a child who has been betrayed by someone in whom he had placed implicit trust.

I had lost the battle before I began it.

# CROSS-CULTURAL COMMUNICATION

The saxophonist had his eyes closed. He pumped his instrument up and down, and every time he bent forward his clean-shaven head caught the light and glinted. The drummer played with a fixed stare, alternately bursting into a series of jerky movements and withdrawing into a rigid trance. Their dark faces illuminated by the reddish glow looked a little sad and their music filled the place with melancholy.

A man at a corner table put down his drink and said, "I am like those Negroes."

"How so darling?" the girl asked lazily.

"They make such a romantic tableau, but they probably live in horrid slums and have fat nagging wives and dozens of squealing brats."

"That's hardly likely, but anyway I don't see the parallel."

"You are being intentionally obtuse." His voice had an edge of irritation.

"Then suppose you explain yours."

"Don't you see, I seem attractive because I come from the exotic East. But what you know of me here is only my outermost skin. The one that wears good clothes and speaks in English about things which are familiar to you, and after an evening of nightclubbing, takes you back to the lovely house precariously balanced on a fashionable hillside."

"Going nightclubbing was your idea, not mine."

"That's not the point."

"You are too subtle for me."

"You can wake up somebody who is fast asleep, but how do you wake up somebody who is only pretending to be asleep?"

"Let's get out of here, shall we? "It's the atmosphere of the place that's getting you down."

Her voice, light and musical, had the easy confidence of someone used to handling varied social situations. As they emerged into the street she linked her arm in his.

"Would you like to see a topless show?" he asked, pointing to a luridly lit sign.

"No," she said laughing. "Unless you would."

He shook his head.

Their footsteps resolutely swallowed up the sidewalk with the clacking of her high heels and the blunter measured tread of his shoes. There were so many people out in the streets that it was like being alone.

"Let's see some Flamenco dancing," she cried brightly. "I love it, don't you?"

"All right."

They settled themselves at a table quite close to the raised stage. At the back of the stage was a wrought-iron arch which had white paper flowers stuck in it. The walls of the nightclub were covered with Spanish travel posters.

"This place looks like a travel bureau," he said glumly.

A spotlight played on the stage and the dancers came on, a full-blown woman with billowing red skirts and a full-throated voice, and a slender black-haired delicate young man with a sugary smile.

"Some of it reminds me of Indian dancing," he said.

He looked at the girl's rapt face. The light of the orange-shaded lamps which lit the room gave her skin a warm glow. Even her ice-blue eyes looked softer than they did in the daytime, and her dark blond head looked sleek and shining.

"You know, you are beautiful," he said.

She smiled at him with a brief exposure of her even white teeth which always looked a little too large for her fine-drawn slender face.

"Where I come from," he said, "there are no hairdressers, and no shops that sell expensive cosmetics."

"Are you implying that it's hairdressers and cosmetics that make me beautiful?" she whispered.

"And my family lives in a rickety old house. The walls haven't seen fresh paint in a hundred years and they have little holes in which bedbugs live. We cook on the floor and eat on the floor and have a cow and a buffalo and their calves sharing the courtyard with us. The whole place smells of cowdung."

Without a word she got up and walked out.

When they were outside she asked furiously, "Don't you know better than to keep on talking when other people want to watch the show and listen to the music?"

"That's all you care about, what people think of you."

"Not what people think of me, what I think of myself. Even if I didn't care what people think of me, I have no right to spoil their fun."

"Oh stop being so moralistic. I am a mannerless clod. That's another thing. In India everyone talks while watching a play or a music and dance recital. We are all mannerless clods. You won't be able to stand us."

"What are you being so unpleasant for?"

"And I forgot to mention the dust and heat. In the summer it gets so hot and dry that your eyelashes burn off your face and your nostrils are always full of dust."

"I didn't know you had a literary flair."

"This is not literary imagination, my sweet. It's the naked truth."

"I believe you are trying to frighten me out of marrying you."

Her smile was a little strained now and she couldn't quite bring off the bantering tone.

"No, but now that the time has come to go back, it has suddenly hit me how difficult it's going to be for you to live in India. Especially for you."

"Why especially for me? Because I am a spoiled rich brat? God, if I had known how guilty you would make me feel because my parents are rich, I might have chosen poorer parents."

"Well, you are rich, and you are spoiled, in a sense. You've always had everything you wanted. Oh I don't mean to say that I was ever deprived of the important things —"

"I am so relieved. I was expecting a description of a grim childhood when you wore rags and ate a meal only every other day."

"Don't mock. There are people who live like that in India. Thousands of them."

"What does that prove? So long as you were not one of them."

"We were still poorer than you can imagine. What seemed like a pretty comfortable life to me would seem like deprivation to you."

"Maybe I wouldn't mind it."

"People always mind being poorer than they are."

"Let's go and get something to eat. You always drink too much and then get gloomy."

"You have an easy explanation for everything."

"Why not?"

"Because it's all wrong. You don't know what you are fighting against."

They drove to an ocean-front restaurant, one of those places which are consciously rustic.

"Are you getting cold feet? Is that it?" she said.

"No, of course not. You have missed my point."

The waiter came and he gave an order of fried jumbo prawns.

"Ah," he said, "sea-food in San Francisco. Something to look back on for the rest of your life."

After the waiter was out of earshot she said, "I have not missed your point at all."

There was not a trace of a smile on her face and her voice was calm and dead. "We are on the same wavelength, friend. I know very well what I am fighting against. You. But now that we understand each other perfectly, there's no need for us to go on fighting, is there?"

She started working the engagement ring off her finger.

"Now wait a minute," he said. "Don't be mad."

"I am not mad."

"All right, you are not mad. So let's eat and then talk about this sensibly."

"You started it, now let's finish it. Now, before we eat. Then maybe we can digest our food better."

She slid the ring across the unpolished wooden table-top. It rolled off the table, landed on the floor and was stopped by the leg of his chair.

"Come, don't be silly," he said. "Put it back on."

She intertwined her fingers and rested her hands on the table.

"Aren't you going to pick it up?" he said.

"It's yours now. You can pick it up if you want it."

He looked at her in amazement, hesitated, then bent down to pick up the ring.

# THE CHILDLESS ONE

"God knows what monster child is growing inside her," Radha's mother-in-law said in the kitchen.

Radha rolled over painfully. Her body was a clumsy burden to move, but if she lay too long in one position her legs became numb. In the kitchen the voices of the two women — Shripati's mother and aunt — went on and on, gloating in whispers, letting an occasional word come out loud enough for Radha to hear. The murmur of the voices and the smell of the food made her sick. She found the smell of methi particularly revolting and was unwise enough to have said so. Naturally, methi was the vegetable most frequently cooked in their kitchen now.

Shripati had said, "It will be better if you go to my mother."

"She hates me," Radha had said. "I am afraid to go to her."

"You will see, it will all be different now. After all, you are going to give her a grandson. For his sake she will treat you well. And it will be better for you to be there, to have someone with you all the time. Here you are all alone when I go to work."

She had still demurred and Shripati had said, "Don't worry so much, Radha. I will come and see you whenever I can. You will be all right."

Finally she had given in, though she had not believed him. What did he know? She knew that her mother-in-law was too nasty to change. Sons never wanted to believe the worst of their mothers. Oh well, the days would fly and in no time she would be back with Shripati. What would her son look like? Or daughter? Not like the grandmother, Radha hoped. That was another thing. Nobody was going to save her from her mother-in-law's wrath if she had a daughter.

183

Radha found that Shripati had been right after all. Her mother-in-law had not actually changed, of course, but she seemed to feel that a certain amount of consideration had to be shown to the mother of her grandson. The consideration was grudgingly shown, and Radha enjoyed it the more because of it. The old woman catered to her slightest whim, whether it was to visit a particular temple or eat a particular food, because she feared that the child might be born defective if the mother's wish remained unfulfilled. Radha even enjoyed the occasional malevolent glance thrown in her direction when the old woman thought she was not looking.

Shripati came for a visit and told his mother when he left, "Look after her well." When he left the mother fumed. "Look after her indeed. What have I been doing all these days but looking after her and fetching and carrying for her? He has a nerve, telling me what to do."

Radha smiled to herself. This was sweet revenge for all the years of being treated like dirt.

When nine months of her pregnancy were over, the old woman asked, "Have you counted right?"

"Of course."

"Well, some women go the full nine months and nine days."

The aunt said, "The first child is often late in coming. Especially if it's a boy."

A few days later Shripati's mother again asked, "Are you sure you counted right?"

"Yes. Let me see, it was Paush —"

They counted and re-counted the months and the days and Radha finally had to admit that she was overdue. When she was almost ten months gone the midwife was called in. She poked Radha here and there and said, "There's time yet."

The swollen abdomen which Radha had carried so proudly was now a focus of pain and fear and shame. At first everyone had said that she looked so big because she carried a son. Then they speculated that perhaps she had twins. Now they avoided her eyes. She knew they talked about her, from the way they suddenly stopped talking when she appeared. She stopped going out, to avoid the women and their ghoulish looks and talk. But she could not avoid her mother-in-law, who went about her work muttering not quite under her breath. When Radha had had enough of hearing the muttering she screamed at the old woman.

"I am sure you have cast an evil eye on my child, you dried-up old bag. Oh I wish I had never listened to Shripati and come here."

"Where would you have gone, eh?" Her mother-in-law stood over her, hands on hips, legs planted wide apart, nostrils flaring with the sheer joy of the fight. "Where would you have gone, I would like to know. You have no home, nor father nor mother. You were just a poor dowryless girl and my son was tricked into marrying you."

"Tricked, you say? Was he a baby at his mother's breast that he could be tricked into marrying anyone? He married me because he saw me and liked me."

"Saw you! Hah! Whoever heard of showing a girl to a bridegroom before getting his parents' approval? It just goes to show what a shameless slut you are and what low-born savages your aunt and uncle are."

"If my uncle is low-born then so are you. After all, he is your cousin."

"Nobody who would play such a dirty trick on me is a cousin of mine." She added in a reasonable, let-me-be-fair voice, "But why should I blame him? Who would want to feed an orphan forever?"

"How dare you call me an orphan when my father is alive?"

The mother-in-law snorted. "That no-good parasite. What use is he to anyone even if he is alive?"

For the time being this silenced Radha. Her father, who had perfected the art of living without working, had sponged off somebody all his life. At first his wife had worked and supported him. After she died, he had lived for a brief period with her brother. Now he lived with his son and the son's shrew of a wife, whose insults he swallowed without protest along with his *bhakri*. Radha would rather die than throw herself on the mercy of her sister-in-law who had a big rock where her heart should have been.

Shripati's aunt was a gentler person. She did not abuse Radha or fight with her. She only told stories in a sad, fatalistic voice. Some woman she knew had to have her belly cut open because her child grew so big that it could not be delivered normally, and then both mother and child died. Another woman had her first child very late in life and it was so retarded that it couldn't even crawl at six. Radha was twenty-three and married seven years.

Shripati came and saw his wife pale and bloated and hardly able to move.

"Why haven't you taken her to a doctor in Satara?" he demanded.

"We called in the midwife," his mother told him.

"What does that stupid woman know about anything?"

"You may be a big policeman in Bombay, Shripati," the old woman's voice trembled with anger. "But I won't have you coming here and shouting at me. If you don't think I am capable of looking after your precious wife, you can take her away. I don't see what you are so worked up about. She is not the first woman in the world to give birth to a child."

Shripati looked somewhat shamefaced by he was not going to let her have the last word while his wife watched the exchange.

"All right, that's enough," he said. "I'm going to Satara to get a taxi. She is too sick to go on the bus. And you had better be ready to go along. She will need someone to stay with her."

At the hospital Shripati listened unbelievingly to the doctor's verdict.

"You mean, it's not a child at all?"

"No, it's a tumor, a growth."

"But everyone said she was pregnant with a child."

The doctor looked pityingly at Shripati. "You people are all the same," he said. "If you had shown her to a proper doctor, you would have known this long ago. She could have been operated on, and needn't have suffered all these months."

"What's to be done now?"

"She will have to have an operation of course. As soon as possible."

"Can you do it?"

"Yes. But if you don't want to spend a lot of money you should take her to the government hospital."

"I have money," Shripati said a little contemptuously.

Radha cried a great deal when he told her all this, but he was so bewildered himself that he had no words with which to console her. He could not believe what the doctor had told him. Even the next morning, when Radha was taken into the operating room, he kept feeling that the doctor must be mistaken.

By the time the operation was over, he had convinced himself that everything was going to be all right and that it was a child after all. It was just that the child could not be born in the normal way and the doctor had to do an operation. He had heard of such cases.

He went in smiling when the doctor sent for him. He did not see Radha anywhere but the doctor was pointing at something rather proudly.

"Do you see that? That's what we took out of your wife. She will be all right now."

The thing lay on an enamel tray on a metal table, and looked like something bought at the butcher's shop. Shripati stood rooted to the floor, staring at the obscene pink-purple hunk. It still seemed to be pulsating, like some horrible freak form of life. Next to it a label was propped up, stating its weight and circumference as though it was a tuber put on display in a

187

vegetable show. This was inside. Radha? No, no, it couldn't be. Someone was playing a horrible joke on him. He felt sick.

Radha was brought home from the hospital, and was slow in regaining her strength. She looked like an old woman, gaunt and frazzle-haired. She wept constantly and asked Shripati to take her to Bombay.

"After you get well," he said.

"I'll get well there."

"Who will look after you until you are well?"

"Don't leave me here. Your mother will kill me if you leave me with her and go away."

"Shut up. How can you say that? Didn't she look after you all these days? And who would care for you now if she weren't here?"

While leaving he told her, "Get well soon. Mother's an old woman now and it tires her to cook and wash for you. You ought to be helping her rather than making more work for her."

Radha cried, "Don't turn against me. I am your wife."

After Shripati had left his mother said, "Some wife, who cannot even give him a child."

Radha wept herself dry and thought, "I've got nobody now. I've only got myself. I must get well quickly." And the next time her mother-in-law brought her a plate of sticky semi-liquid rice, she pushed the plate away and said, "I don't want this child's food. Give me some *bhakri*. I want to get well and strong quickly."

Her mother-in-law brought her some *bhakri* and laughed and said, "It won't do you any good, because you will never have any children no matter what you eat."

"That's a lie."

"Ask the doctor. That's what he said, that you can't have any children. Shripati has no use for you now."

"You are making it up, you vile old woman."

Radha heard people come and go, strange voices discuss and argue and agree. She said, "You can't do this. Shripati can't marry again. It's against the law."

"Who is going to worry about the law? Shripati is a policeman."

"He won't marry again, just because you say so."

"Won't he?"

"It's a sin to make bad blood between a husband and wife, to break up a marriage."

The old woman smiled and said, "Keep your mouth shut, if you know what's good for you, or I'll kill you and then it won't be against the law for him to marry."

Shripati showed himself quite willing to remarry and Radha, afraid for her life, left her mother-in-law's house. She found work as a farm labourer with a *bagaitdar* a few miles away.

Every day she went to the temple near the *basti* where she lived in a hut, and promised Bhairobaba various offerings if he gave Shripati and his mother the punishment they deserved. In the *basti* she became something a joke. She told everyone her story, and her uncontrolled rage and repertoire of abusive words caused much amusement among the others. They called 'vedi', mad woman, and baited her to fill an empty hour.

"If Shripati comes here," they said, "what will you do with him? Cut him up into pieces and eat him with your *bhakri?*"

"He would poison my insides if I ate him."

At first this sort of talk offered her a release and gave her a strange kind of comfort. But then she grew tired of being used for a few laughs. She learned to keep herself to herself. Life assumed a fairly placid routine and she began to live without hatred and bitterness as her constant companions.

And then suddenly one day, long after she had stopped talking about him or thinking about him, Shripati appeared. He came into her hut and for a few moments she didn't know what to say. Finally she asked him how he was, rather formally. He said he was all right and added, "You don't look so well."

She knew that hard work in the sun had aged her, darkened and wrinkled her skin and burned the lustre out of her eyes. The false concern in his voice angered her.

"I am well enough," she said.

She looked at him, still handsome and young looking, with the sleekness of city living on him.

"And how is your old woman?" she asked.

"She is all right."

"That's not what I heard. I heard that she is sick and your wife lives with her and looks after her." She shook her head and said, "Poor girl. I don't envy her. I'd rather weed in the fields all day."

"Is this why you asked to see me, so you could insult me?" he shouted.

"I never asked to see you."

"That's what Gena told me."

It was then that she heard the men's hushed voices outside and understood. "Gena," she cried, "you wait until I get my hands on you."

Shripati was getting up to leave.

"Wait," she said. "Now that you are here, there is something I want to show you."

She raised her voice and called, "Mahadya, come in here."

A small dirty child waddled in on rickety legs and stood looking impassively at the stranger, sucking on a thumb.

"Who is he?" Shripati asked.

"He is my son."

Shripati laughed. "Which dung heap did you pick him up from?"

"I didn't pick him up from anywhere. He was born of me."

"Have you no shame?"

190

"Why should I have shame? What can a woman do when her husband isn't man enough to protect her from wolves?"

"You filthy whore! Whose son is he?"

"He is not yours, that's for sure." She started laughing.

"Shut up."

"When are you going to marry again, Shripati? How many times will you marry before you know that you will never have any children?"

He turned haughtily and walked out of the hut. She screamed after him, "All you were ever fit to father was a lump of flesh, do you hear? A child with neither head nor limbs."

# THE DEATH OF A HERO

"Sit down," the principal said. But Mr. Tagde continued to stand, gaining courage from his own straight-backed stance, because he was beginning to feel a little afraid now.

The principal looked unhappy. He disliked being forced to perform this sort of an unpleasant task.

"I wish you would consider withdrawing this report," he said.

"I am sorry, sir, I cannot do that," Mr. Tagde said. He was pleased with his own unwavering voice and uncompromising words.

"It will be a very damaging report if put on record."

"It is a factual report on very damaging conduct."

"You are asking for the boy's expulsion from school. Don't you think the punishment is too harsh for a few boyish pranks?"

"He has spoiled benches in my classroom by scoring them with a razor blade. He has made the blackboard useless by scratching on it with a piece of tin. He has broken several windowpanes by throwing stones at them while class was in session. Yesterday he broke another one and the flying pieces of glass hurt one of the pupils badly. That is not all. Many students have complained of having their books, notebooks, pens stolen, and I can get evidence that Morey is behind it. There have been complaints from girl students that he stops them on the street and shouts obscenities at them and threatens to beat them up if they complain. I cannot agree with you that all this can be called mere boyish pranks."

The principal spread his hands in a helpless gesture. He looked at Mr. Tagde, a small thin man in his slightly yellowed dhoti and his coat of a nondescript colour and his black cap. Outwardly he looked the same as he had for the past fifteen years that the principal had known him. A conscientious teacher, a mature and rational man, suitably diplomatic in his dealing with those in authority, a good man to work with.

Heartened by his scrutiny of his colleague, the principal continued more hopefully, "But the boy has already been punished for his misconduct. Why rake it all up again?"

"When Morey hurt that boy yesterday — the glass cut his cheek, and small pieces of it had to be removed from the wound at the dispensary — I decided that he had to be stopped before he did any further damage. The boy who was hurt comes from a poor family. His parents are not in a position to do anything about Morey."

"I am sure Veerendra did not mean this particular boy any harm."

"You are right, sir. He did not. He merely wanted to break a windowpane and disrupt my class. If in the process someone got hurt, that was an added bonus."

Mr. Tagde surprised himself by the sudden intensity of his anger. The kind of anger he had felt when he saw the irregular star of the broken window and the blood running down the boy's cheek, an anger which sends the blood rushing to one's eyes and momentarily blurs one's vision and one's fear.

"There is no call to be sarcastic, Mr. Tagde," the principal said sharply. "I am not condoning the boy's behaviour. I am merely suggesting that you are putting too serious a construction on it."

Mr. Tagde neither moved nor spoke.

"I could refuse to put the matter on the agenda for the school committee meeting, you know."

"Then I shall have no alternative but to send a copy of the report to each committee member and one to Vartavihar."

This was an extempore thought, and his elation on having stumbled on it gave Mr. Tagde more confidence.

The principal made a feeble attempt at laughing. "Come now, you don't mean it," he said. "You wouldn't want to drag the name of our school through the papers."

"I meant every word I said."

"You are aware," the principal said, carefully enunciating each word as though to make sure Mr. Tagde heard it, "that the chairman of the school committee is Veerendra's uncle?"

"I am."

"You still want this report to go up to the committee?"

"Yes."

"All right, then I shall forward it as your personal recommendation, for consideration at the meeting to be held on Friday evening."

That's right, save your own skin, don't endorse it, Mr. Tagde thought, looking with distaste at the principal's bland face. Then he thought, I have no right to be bitter. I spent my life doing just what he is doing, saving my own skin.

While he was walking home, the enormity of what he had done began to dawn on him. He had always had access to all the facts of course. He had simply failed to combine them and realize their implications. Without the principal's endorsement, his report would cause serious repercussions. It might very well mean the loss of his job. There were rules for the protection of employees of long standing. But mofussil private schools had a way of getting around rules.

He decided that he would simply have to face the consequences. The loss of his job would not be such a great tragedy. He was only three years away from retirement anyway. His children were on their own, a daughter married and two sons in good jobs. For once in his life he was in a position to do something he felt was right, without fear of consequences. He was sick of doing the bidding of the petty politicians and manoeuvrers who ran the school, and of always being afraid of losing his job if he punished or failed their delinquent children. There had to come a time in every man's life when he had to square all these things with his conscience.

When he reached home he called out as usual, "I am home." While he removed his coat and had a wash, his wife would have a cup of tea ready for him. He debated telling her about what had happened, but discarded the idea. He had always been thankful for her unquestioning acceptance of his decisions, though her acceptance had meant only that she was not sufficiently interested. Since this decision might affect her, it might interest her. But for the time being he was content to leave it.

The reactions came sooner than he expected. Mr. Thakar, the lawyer, brought up the subject during their before-dinner walk.

"Principal Deshpande asked me to have a talk with you."

Mr. Tagde said, "I have made my decision and nothing you say is going to change it."

Mr. Thakar looked at his friend in surprise.

"Wait till you hear what I have to say," he said, holding up his hand. "I hold no brief for Veerendra Morey. He is despicable and deserves to be kicked out of school. The point is this. You know and I know that your report is not going to serve that purpose, because of circumstances you are very well aware of. Then why commit suicide needlessly?"

"I know you have only my interests at heart, and I am thankful for it. But it's no use your trying to talk me out of this. I have made up my mind."

"But why?"

"I think this whole system is rotten, by which politicians control educational institutions. Somebody has to strike out against it."

"Why you?"

"Why not me? Because I am just a poor insignificant teacher?"

Mr. Thakar sighed. "Think of the consequences. First, you may lose your job."

195

"I wouldn't mind. I can continue to make a living by giving tuitions. That was what I had planned to do after my retirement anyway."

"Do you think it would be easy for you to get tuitions if you declare yourself openly an enemy of the Moreys?"

Mr. Tagde was silent a long time. This was a logical possibility, but it had not occurred to him.

"Everybody in this town is afraid of them," he said finally. "I know that. But there are other places one can go to."

"You mean you are prepared to disarrange your whole life over this worthless boy?"

"Yes."

"Well, I admire you, Tagde, but I still think you are making a foolish mistake."

Vishnupant Joshi came to see him the next morning. A large, aggressively hearty man, a brahmin *bagaitdar*, careful of his skin but foxy enough to gain a foothold in Maratha politics, and therefore the ideal pacifier and go-between.

Over tea Mr. Tagde said, "Why should a father's money and political power protect his child from punishment which he richly deserves?"

Every time he argued his case, he seemed to receive an inner reinforcement from his own words.

"I agree with you, it shouldn't. But the fact is that it does. It does all the time, all over the world. We have to live with it. That's life. You have to keep your balance. Why jeopardize your position for a fine-sounding sentiment?"

"We are looking at the question from opposing points of view, Mr. Joshi, and I cannot hope to make you understand mine."

"Don't be in a hurry to take a stand. Think about it for a while. There is still time to withdraw your report."

"You can take it as final that I will not withdraw it. If necessary, I am prepared to hand in my resignation."

"Are you aware that the school committee has powers to stop your pension?"

"I was not aware of it until you mentioned it," Mr. Tagde said in cold anger. "If you came here to ensure my compliance through threats, you are wasting your time."

On Wednesday night when Mr. Tagde was returning home from a visit to the public lavatory which he used, he was attacked by a group of boys. They beat him with sticks and stones and fists. He thought he recognized Veerendra Morey's voice urging the others to "teach the bastard a lesson".

The next morning, covered with turmeric paste and bandages, unable to get up, Mr. Tagde lay in bed groaning with pain.

The night before when he walked in after the beating, his wife had been horrified and said angrily, "Why won't you take back your silly report? Is it worth being beaten, losing your job? Oh yes, I know what's going on, even if you won't tell me anything."

"I think it's worth it," he said calmly.

"They will kill you."

"Let them. I am an old man, I am not afraid of dying."

"You think only of yourself. What about me? What will happen to me if you die? I shall be a helpless widow for nothing."

Mr. Tagde felt like laughing. He said gently, "Not for nothing, my dear. For a principle."

"What good will a principle be to me when I am a widow?"

Then he did laugh, and she withdrew into sullenness which she had not abandoned with the dawning of the next day. Watching her going about her work silently, he thought, I cannot be bothered with inessentials now. I have jumped into this, and I have to see it to the end. God will look after me, and look after her if something does happen to me.

The neighbours had seen him limping home with a bloody face, so the news must be all over town, but nobody came to see

197

him. This is what I shall have to get used to, he thought with a strange kind of exaltation. I shall have to stand alone. He thanked God for giving him this opportunity to become free of fear at last, to grow into a tall, proud man.

In the evening Mr. Thakar came.

"Glad to see you," Mr. Tagde said. "I thought you had also abandoned me, like the others."

"Ha-ha, you do get funny ideas."

Mr. Tagde frowned at the lawyer's levity in the face of the seriousness of the situation.

"I bring you news," Mr. Thakar said.

"Good or bad?" Mr. Tagde asked cautiously.

"That depends on you."

"If you are going to ask me to back out, you can save your breath."

"At least let me tell you everything before you jump to conclusions. When I heard about your getting beaten up, I said to myself, this has gone too far. Something must be done. So I went to Ramrao Morey, Veerendra's uncle. I put it to him that you were not going to withdraw your report no matter what, and many of the townspeople respected you for it; that the beating you had received was disgraceful and sufficient evidence, if any was needed, that your report is accurate; that the beating, if no action was taken about it, would create a lot of resentment in town. Finally I said that if he looked at the thing rationally — I emphasized the point that I felt he was the only member of their family who was fully capable of thinking rationally — being kicked out of school might be the best thing that could happen to Veerendra. He agreed."

"What?" Mr. Tagde shot up in bed.

"Calm yourself. Of course he did not agree that Veerendra should be kicked out of school. He agreed that it would do Veerendra good to be taken out of school and put in a boarding school such as the Morgiri Boys' School which is run specially for problem boys. Naturally the family has not been happy about Veerendra's exploits, but they haven't known how to control him. I also brought it to Ramrao's attention that, in view of the forthcoming elections in which Veerendra's father is a candidate, any adverse publicity — such as you, I said, were capable of giving this matter — would be undesirable at this time. She he consulted with Veerendra's father and they have agreed to take the boy out of school immediately, and in June, only three months from now, send him away. This of course on condition that you withdraw your report about the boy immediately. You will have to agree that it is a fair compromise, because it gives you what you want."

Mr. Tagde, white and trembling, sank back on his pillow.

"What is the matter?" Mr. Thakar asked in alarm. "Are you feeling ill?"

"No, no. I am all right. It's just that — this is such a surprise."

"I understand. After the tension of the last few days, it must be a sudden relief. You do agree, don't you? I have to get in touch with Mr. Morey and let him know tonight."

Mr. Tagde nodded mechanically and then closed his eyes; a tired old teacher looking ahead to three more years of teaching and then retirement and a pension, however measly.

# THE LOTUS LEAVES

Hirabai stood on the high platform in the grape garden. Her sun-burnished brown arm was poised against the sky, the sling-shot taut in her hand. She gave another of her complicated bird-scaring cries. The cry began with a cajoling, crooning sound, something like a dove's call. Then she started scolding. Gradually the scolding became louder and harsher until it culminated in a hysterical shriek. Then her voice came down several notes and her call ended on a pleading, husky-sweet note.

William Levin had been busy snapping pictures.

"Don't waste all your film on her," Sarojini said. "You can't buy any here."

"Oh I have plenty. She really is magnificent."

"Even so you mustn't stare at her. You are embarrassing her. You Americans are so funny. You find the strangest things interesting."

"Don't you think she is wonderful?"

"Nothing is wonderful when you are close to it day after day."

"You don't like it much here, do you?"

The casual interest in his voice stung her. It's safe to get enthusiastic about Hirabai, she thought. He can admire her openly, take pictures of her, stare at her. But I am different. Genteel people don't show interest in each other, only in their social inferiors. In another age he would have had Hirabai brought to his room at night, and he would have paid her well in the morning if she had happened to please him. Like the English — the conquering white heroes sleeping with the lowliest and filthiest women and leaving a progeny of half-breeds of whom nobody is proud. But I am not quite accurate there. The woman's people were so humble that they were proud even of this. Sarojini thought of the fair-skinned, blue-eyed blonde girl in the sweepers' colony, perhaps some district collector's daughter or grand-daughter, collecting the town's excreta. Little Saheb's daughter, they called her.

"Why don't you like it here?" Levin asked her again.

"It's all right, but not a place where I look forward to spending my whole life."

"How do you keep busy here?"

"I don't."

"Aren't you interested in Pratap's work?"

"I was in the beginning," she smiled. "All the other farmers we know live in town. But that wasn't good enough for us. We had to have the real thing. Pratap was just back from America, and he was full of ideas. It seemed so glamorous to live right on the farm. I was just as eager as he was. I had never thought of a career of my own and it seemed enough of a career to throw myself into his work. But I couldn't keep up the interest. Farming is so dull after all. Year after year you go through the same routine. And unless you have a dream to sustain you, routine can kill you."

"What about Pratap?"

"He thrives on it. He is very happy here. But it's not a dream that sustains him."

"What is it, then?"

"A sense of pride maybe. And the longer he lives here the deeper his roots will go. He will feel lost anywhere else. That's the sort of person he is."

"It makes things difficult for you, I expect."

She gave a wry smile. "We have nothing outside this. Pratap is friendly, but he doesn't need friends, or even just people to talk to. He doesn't need any entertainment either, so long as he is busy. It gets so lonely here, sometimes I wish I could go away and never come back."

"Why don't you?"

"That wouldn't help. I have never really thought in terms of making a separate life for myself. I don't know if I can."

"You could give it a try."

"It would be awful to have to come back with my tail between my legs, wouldn't it? Besides, there is Pratap."

Levin shrugged and put his hands in his pocket.

"Sometimes," Sarojini said, "I feel the world is so full of promise, but I am not in it."

"Isn't this part of the world?"

"A very small part."

"Nobody can have the whole world."

She heard the slight impatience in his voice — the impatience of a man for a child who is incapable of grasping simple truths. They walked in silence for a while and it was she who opened the conversation again.

"Did you know Pratap in the States?"

"No, he was a friend of my brother's. When Bob knew I was coming to this part of India he gave me your address. I didn't think I would get here actually, but then I heard about this festival of the horses, and realized that the town where it takes place would be close to where you are."

"Our visitors always come here for a reason. The majority of them are friends and relatives from the city who think spending a holiday on a real farm is the thing to do. They don't come to see us."

"I must plead guilty. But whatever the reason for my visit, I am happy that it gave me a chance of meeting you."

He gave a formal little bow.

"Tell me," he said, "where does that woman live? The birdscarer?"

Sarojini tried not to show her disappointment at the sudden change of subject.

"Near here," she said. "Why do you want to know?"

"I am just curious to know how she lives, what she thinks about, what makes her tick."

"I wonder if she will be flattered to know you are curious about her. Probably not. I always used to attribute personality to these people. They were different from anyone else I had met. The salt of the earth. The idea is more interesting than the people, though. Once you get to know them you find there's nothing more to them than what's on the surface. They are like sheep. All alike. Inert, ignorant, poor. And people who are that ignorant and that poor aren't interesting."

Looking at him, she knew she had shocked him.

She said, "Let's go in, shall we? I can't stand too much sun."

"Of course."

She looked sideways at his sunburned face and neck. It had turned an unattractive blotchy red. At the hairline his skin still showed white.

"What is the programme for this afternoon?" she asked.

"I think we'll start right after lunch, if you don't mind. I want to catch the procession at the starting point. Then we'll walk along with it, talk to people, take pictures. I have some background information on the festival, but talking to people gives you an insight into what it means to them. That's where I need you. Unless you would rather put me in touch with another interpreter."

He said it as though it didn't matter to him one way or the other.

"I shall be delighted to be of help. It will be something interesting for me to do. For a change."

He gave a little one-sided smile.

"Sometimes," he said, "by calling life dull you can make it seem more so than it actually is."

"That can work the other way too. Sometimes you can fool yourself into thinking life is significant when it isn't."

"It wouldn't matter if you did."

"Wouldn't it?"

Pratap lent Levin his motorcycle.

"You are sure you don't want to come?" Levin asked him.

"I'm too busy, Bill. I have to supervise the packing and despatching of the grapes."

"He thinks the world will stop going round unless he personally supervises its revolutions every minute of the day," Sarojini said.

Pratap laughed. The sun had tanned his face a beautiful polished brown and his teeth looked very white when he laughed. Sarojini, in a moment of swift wistfulness, tried to imagine him in Levin's place but couldn't.

"Enjoy yourself, darling," Pratap said. "You don't have much fun here."

Levin kicked the bike into life. After they had been riding a few minutes he said, shouting over his shoulder, "So he admits you have no fun here."

"Oh yes, readily. But he thinks I should accept it as an inevitable part of my life here. Some things you can have, some you can't. It's that simple."

"A very sensible attitude."

"Now you are laughing at me."

"Not at all. I seriously think it's a sensible attitude, if you can manage it."

"I take it you are one of those who can. Like Pratap."

"I flatter myself that I am."

In the morning he had smelled nice, a spicy sweet smell of talcum powder and after-shave lotion. But now he smelled stale and unpleasant. His shirt already had a dark smudge around the collar. He probably washes it himself at night, she thought. Drip-dry, wrinkle-free. A shirt to suit his temperament.

"Are you married?" she asked him.

He laughed. "No."

"Why did you laugh?"

204

"I wondered when you were going to get around to asking that. A woman never feels she has been properly introduced to a man until she knows his marital status."

"I didn't mean to pry. I am sorry."

"Don't be."

She wanted to ask him if there was a girl back home to whom he wrote love letters. But after his laughter she didn't.

When they reached town he parked the motorbike and they found their way to the Krishna temple, the headquarters of the Krishnabhakta sect. The procession was just starting, and Levin got a good shot of the men carrying the brass horses emerging from the temple. The Krishnabhaktas, a sect founded by a man born in these parts, had flourished for a few hundred years. Though there were followers of the sect scattered all over India, this town — the Krishna temple which was said to have been built over the spot where Krishna had revealed himself to the founder, and the *math* connected with it where the current head of the sect lived — had remained the centre of pilgrimage for them. Hundreds of them converged here for this festival.

Several drummers dressed in saffron and white led the procession. Levin and Sarojini joined in. She got into a conversation with a man who walked alongside of them. After talking to him for a few minutes, she turned to Levin. "He gives a very fanciful explanation of the origin of this festival. Do you want it?"

"Oh yes, I want all the information I can get. Later I will discuss it with my collaborator and we might decide to weed out some of it. But it's important that I get it all. Often the sources from which I get my background information don't mention all the legends associated with these festivals, mostly because the legends get started after the festival is already well established."

"Well, this man traces the origin of this one to seven hundred years ago, when a shepherd who was going back from a pilgrimage was crossing this river. Suddenly his horse stopped in midstream. Nothing the shepherd tried budged the horse. Finally he prayed to God Krishna, and as suddenly as he had stopped, the horse moved. The horse temple was built on the spot where the horse unaccountably stopped. The story is also supposed to explain the custom of the followers of the sect to offer a brass horse to the god in order to have their wishes fulfilled. On the morning of the festival a puja is offered to the horses and then they are taken in procession to the horse temple and brought back."

Levin was furiously taking notes in a little notebook. "Excellent," he said. "Now let's move on and verify that story from a couple more people."

You are so cool and clinical about it, she thought. For the time being the end and aim of your actions is your book. By William Levin and whoever. Describing in detail the pagan ritual and the ignorance and superstition and stupidity of my people. Why don't you leave us alone and find something else to take to pieces? The willingness of the people to give information to this foreigner made her ears burn with anger. They are so ignorant, so without pride. Why don't they tell him to mind his own business?

More people had joined the procession and, walking in the thick of it, she kept being pushed against Levin. A couple of times she glanced at him but he was busy watching or taking notes or focusing his camera. Once when she stumbled he automatically took her arm and steadied her.

Perhaps, she thought angrily, it is a conspiracy of men to keep women on the fringe of their lives.

The procession stopped every few yards. At every stop people put *kumkum* powder and flowers on the horses. Someone kept scattering handfuls of *gulal* among the drummers. Their dark faces were covered with the bright pink powder and their hot eyes shone through the pink with a demented light as they danced and beat the drums with increasing frenzy.

They were now in the parched riverbed and the sand threw off the blazing brightness of the summer sun. There was a group of women walking behind the horses and they now formed the focus of interest. There were more than a dozen of them. They began to sway and rock in time to the drumbeat, and periodically interrupted their rocking to sit down or stand in a rigid trance or weep with abandoned sobs. In the middle of the sand and dry mud there was a deep water hole. When the procession reached this, the women screamed and threw themselves into it and then, climbing out, rolled around in the riverbed until their clothes and faces were covered with soft mud.

"People don't seem to agree about these women," Sarojini said. "Some say it is a sign of the presence of God in them. One man said that mad people belonging to the sect come here from all over India. They believe that they can be cured if the head of the sect blesses them on this day. But the man who told me this is not a member of the sect. The others don't agree with him. They insist it is a manifestation of some divine power. I must say, it doesn't look very divine to me."

"That's because you have preconceived ideas of what divine should be."

"One man, who seems a bit more sophisticated than the others, claims that if we went closer and heard what they are saying, we would find that the women scream the most shocking abuse. They abuse the founder of the sect, and this man says that it expresses the agony of their religious search."

"Fascinating."

"The onlookers, who mostly don't belong to the sect but come from outlying villages to watch the procession, think there is something sinister about the women. It is believed they can put a curse on people. Do you really think they are mad?"

"Difficult to say. Possibly it's a self-induced frenzy which feeds on itself. If I started going through all those gyrations, I should end up in a frenzy too."

He smiled and his smile made a fellow-conspirator of her. It annoyed her because he was right. She felt as much of an alien as he did in this world of religious frenzy. But she didn't return his smile.

"It's rather frightening, isn't it?" she said. "Such abandon makes you think of the human being under the skin. It's unholy."

"Many religious phenomena seem unholy."

"Have you seen anything like this in any of the other festivals you visited?"

"I've seen equally odd things."

The procession emerged out of the riverbed and turned back towards the starting point. They had been walking for close to three hours.

Sarojini looked at the saffron and pink and vermilion drummers. The white in their dress was all but invisible. They still beat the drums with apparently undiminished energy. She looked at the mad women, their hair streaming all over their faces, staring unseemingly into the crowds which now thickly lined the streets. The shining brass horses bore streaks of red. Heat and light and colour became one and exploded somewhere behind her eyes. In spite of the sun she shivered a little.

"Do you mind if I leave you for a while?" she asked Levin. "I'm afraid the sun has been too much for me."

He was instantly solicitous.

"Heavens, I am sorry. I should have remembered. Is there anywhere you can go and rest? I'll take you there."

"Oh no, I wouldn't think of letting you miss this. I'll just sit under that tree over there. Are you sure you can do without me?"

"Of course. I have everything I need. I only want to take a few more pictures while the light is still right. Then I'll join you."

"Take your time. I'm in no hurry."

Her head ached and her eyes burned, and in the cool shade of the tree she fell asleep.

When she opened her eyes Levin was sitting by her.

"How long have you been here? Why didn't you wake me?" she said. She didn't like the idea that he had been watching her sleep.

"I thought I owed you a rest after having been so inconsiderate. Do you feel all right?"

"Oh yes, I am fine now. Doesn't the sun and the heat bother you?"

"Not much." He looked almost purple-red now.

"Is the procession over?"

"Yes. I found you were asleep so I went back and saw it to the bitter end." He laughed. He had the glow of the man with a job well done.

She felt dull with her long nap. Dull also with the feeling of a day somehow wasted, or at least ill-used.

"Shall we go home?" she asked.

"I brought you some tea and bananas."

"Wonderful. How did they let you bring the glasses?"

"I paid for them."

She couldn't help a smile.

"They probably made you pay four times what the glasses are worth."

"Never mind."

They sipped the now lukewarm tea and ate through half a dozen bananas.

"Will you leave tomorrow?" she asked.

"Yes."

"I suppose we shall never see you again. We don't have another unusual festival to offer you."

"I want to thank you," he said without answering her implied question, "for your hospitality and help."

"That has such a final sound. Tell me, what is it that makes you invulnerable?"

209

He watched the horizon silently. The sun had started on the downward path and its light was diffused with all the dust in the air.

"I am not invulnerable," he said. "Not really."

He got up without giving her a chance to say anything further.

"It's nearly dark," he said. "Time we went back."


That evening after dinner Pratap and Levin sat talking for a long time on the screened verandah. It was one of those still summer nights which are unwilling to let the day's heat go. The sour-sweet smell of over-ripe grapes lay heavy on the air. Sarojini lay on her bed fully dressed and thought how much she hated the smell. It was all around her, like a wall.

Presently she heard the men say their good nights. She heard Levin go to his room and Pratap go out. He would take his last round of the day, making sure everything was all right. She got up and straightened her sari. Standing before the mirror, she smoothed her hair.

She felt flushed with the heat and her heart pounded with the effort of breathing as she knocked on Levin's door.

"Come in," he said.

"I thought you might need some water. It's a warm night."

"Thank you."

She put the water jug and glass on the bedside table.

"You certainly found a lot to say to each other, you and Pratap."

"We did, as a matter of fact. Why didn't you join us?"

She shrugged. There was nothing more to say. She just stood there, compelling him to meet her eyes. When he looked at her, there was something in his eyes which sent a little thrill of fear through her. She walked into the arms he held out for her.

And then suddenly the overpowering smell of his unwashed body, the demanding pressure of his arms, his lips, became something to fight against. She pushed away from his suffocating nearness, and was surprised to see how easily his arms released her.

Her nostrils hurt with the dry hot air as she drew a long breath to steady her voice.

"Good night Bill," she said.

"Good night."

She didn't wait to see whether he was angry with her or laughing at her. She didn't care.

She had suddenly arrived at the knowledge of how Little Saheb's daughters happened.

When she returned to her bedroom Pratap was getting ready for bed.

"Did anyone put a jug of water in Bill's room?" he asked.

"That's what I was doing."

"Good. I thought you would be in bed by now. Did you have a nice day?"

"So-so. You know, our friend Bill is enamoured of Hirabai." Pratap laughed.

"Everyone to his taste," he said.

She allowed herself to be pulled into his familiar perfunctory arms.

"Ah, I am tired tonight," he said. "We sent two hundred boxes of grapes today and there are at least that many still waiting to be harvested tomorrow. What do you think of that?"

She smiled in the darkness.

"Nice," she said.